PRAISE FOR *The Dirty Parts of the Bible*

"While the title suggests a raunchy read, this rich and soulful novel is actually a rather well-done coming-of-age tale steeped in wanderlust and whimsy. The author does an excellent job in making well-charted territory (riding the rails; scavenged campfire meals under the stars) seem vibrant and new. Snippets of scripture, Southern spirituals, and folk ballads lend context and flavor to the text. Most impressive are the jangly dialogue and the characters' distinctive voices, which are authentic and earthy."

— *Publishers Weekly*

"*The Dirty Parts of the Bible* might just be the long-awaited Great American Novel. We experience the odyssey of a young man who searches for lost treasure, his identity, and the alchemy of transforming lust to love. We are enchanted by a young woman who, like the land itself, is protected by the spirit of an Indian warrior. We meet a Socrates-invoking hobo who tells us that 'myths and fairy tales aren't lies—they're deeper truths.' That just about sums up the essence—and magic—of this brilliant book."

—**JOHN M. PERKINS**
New York Times bestselling author

The hobo songs on pages 99–100 are adapted from
Beggars of Life: A Hobo Autobiography by Jim Tully.
The poems on pages 103 and 247 are adapted
from the works of Henry Longfellow.
All song lyrics quoted are in the public domain.

www.amazon.com/author/samtorode
www.facebook.com/SamTorodeBooks
www.dirtypartsofthebible.com

THE DIRTY PARTS OF THE BIBLE

A NOVEL

SAM TORODE

THE ONLY TIME my mother ever swore—or so I was told—was the day I was born. According to Granny, Mama would have made a sailor blush. I weighed nine pounds and had the biggest head of any baby the midwife had ever delivered. "God damn it all to hell!" she yelled, grabbing Father by the collar. "You will never touch me again, you son of a bitch!"

Which explains why I don't have any siblings—and a whole lot else besides.

I was named Tobias after my great grandfather, the original Tobias Henry, who left Kentucky and settled in

Texas sometime in the mid-1800s. That's where I was born, though I have no memories of my first years in Texas; my father moved us to Michigan when I was three. But somehow, someday, I was destined to return. Maybe it was the spirit of old Tobias in my blood.

Or maybe I felt drawn back to Texas because I hated Michigan winters. We lived north of Grand Rapids, in a little town called Remus, where my father was the Baptist pastor. I had good reasons for hating winter—for one thing, I'd have to trudge to the outhouse through four feet of snow. And, once I got to the outhouse, I couldn't sit down or my ass would freeze to the seat.

But Father loved winter. Not Christmastime, mind you, but the dead of winter—that bleak stretch between January and March when old folks lose the will to live. Being a pastor, it was booming business for my father; but it wasn't just the funerals that made him love winter. What he relished was the chance to discipline the flesh, to bring the passions under the Spirit's control. "Warm weather pampers a body," he'd say. "But winter mortifies the flesh and invigorates the soul. There's nothing like a brisk, biting wind to fend off gluttony and lust."

I could see his point: it's hard to fornicate when your balls are frostbitten.

Easter Sunday, 1936, was one of those sumptuous spring mornings Father warned against. Before my parents were out of bed, I headed out to Leach Lake. I was raised never to fish on Sunday and I knew I was heaping God's wrath upon my head, but I had my reasons.

The air at the lake was sweet with the scent of grass and mud. Dragonflies were swooping in locked pairs. Sunfish were cavorting on their sandy beds. Frogs were humping in the muck. Crawdads were doing whatever it is crawdads do. All of nature seemed caught up in a carnival of love—except for me. I sat on a carpet of matted, yellow weeds, snapping twigs between my fingers and longing for Emily Apple.

Emily. I'd loved that girl since the third grade, when she was gangly, buck-toothed, and freckle-faced. What was it about her that pierced my heart? It wasn't sexual. Heck, our chests were the same size.

That changed in seventh grade. As the girls in our class started looking more womanly, Emily exceeded them all. She'd stand at the blackboard multiplying and dividing numbers, while my mouth gaped open—enthralled by the way her cotton dress clung to her budding breasts. And just to think: I was the boy who'd discovered her first.

But, within a year or two, it became apparent that all my affections meant nothing. Emily's new-sprung charms attracted older boys like bees to honey. Boys who had jobs. And money. And drove cars. I didn't have a chance.

I kept hope alive all through high school, while Emily dated Lars Lundgren, a big Nordic bastard with more hair under one armpit than I had on my whole body. Lars was two years older than me. By the spring of '36, he was an all-American in football and track at Northern Michigan. In April, Emily accepted his proposal.

Lars was coming home for Easter, and he and Emily were set to announce their engagement that morning. Which is why I was skipping church to go fishing. Easter or not, damned if I was going to sit in the pew behind them while Lars draped his sweaty arm around her shoulder.

Every night for I don't know how many years, I'd prayed that God would make Emily mine. He hadn't kept up his end of the bargain, I figured—why should I keep up mine? Then and there, on the banks of Leach Lake, I vowed never again to waste another breath in prayer.

While I was busy apostatizing, my father was preaching his Easter sermon. I didn't need to be in church to know what he was preaching about; it was the same thing every Sunday.

"You may call yourself a Christian," he'd say, "but

if you keep a bottle of liquor or a deck a cards in your cupboard, you might as well be a pagan. And don't try to tell me you keep that whiskey for medicinal purposes only. Would you have the devil for your doctor?"

My father, the Reverend Malachi Henry, was a fierce opponent of liquor, dancing, gambling, whoring, and all other forms of worldly enjoyment. He reminded me of a military general as he paced back and forth behind the pulpit, firing off Bible verses like bullets.

After hitting the easy targets—gambling and drinking—he'd set his sights on more subtle evils, like dancing. "Why, it's nothing more than rutting set to music. I can't describe to you what passes under the name of dancing today. You might say, 'But preacher, here in Remus we only have square dances.' Well, a square dance might start innocent, but it sure don't take long to cut off the corners."

Father hadn't always been so grim. He taught me to fish when I was a boy, and my happiest memories of childhood are of the two of us at the lake. But his "moods," as Mama called them, had grown worse over the past few years. To get out from under his dark cloud, I started going fishing alone.

Whenever I needed to clear my head, I lit out for the lake. I never liked exploring the woods like other boys.

To me, a forest is just a bunch of trees, but lakes and rivers are alive. Water is to the land what blood is to the body.

I never learned to hunt because Father thought it was unseemly for a preacher to carry a gun. By Remus standards, I might as well have been born without a penis. (The fact that Remus rhymes with penis was an endless source of amusement for my friends and me. It was our *only* source of amusement.)

Remus was a timber town in its heyday, but the timber ran out in the '20s. Most of the loggers moved to Detroit to work in the auto factories. Those who hung on lived in shanties or shacks of their own making. For these men, there wasn't anything else to do besides hunt. Walking across town any given day, I'd see five or ten deer strung up from trees, their innards all hanging out. If not for the deer, the men would have shot each other for sport.

Michigan is a long way from Glen Rose, Texas, where my parents grew up. Why did Father move us? He claimed that the Spirit had called him. I figured he'd dragged Mama and me north to torture us.

Maybe Remus was the only town that would take him. Down south, most places already had a surplus of Baptist pastors. Texas's main exports are cotton, oil, and preachers.

Why did Father leave the family farm and get into the preaching racket? Here's how he tells it: One morning when he was milking, a cow kicked him upside the head. As he lay on his back staring up at the sky, the clouds parted and Jesus himself appeared.

JESUS: Malachi!
MALACHI: Yes, Lord?
JESUS: I want you to preach.
MALACHI: But I don't know how.
JESUS: Go to the seminary.
MALACHI: The cemetery?
JESUS: No—the *seminary*. Fort Worth Baptist Seminary.

You'd think that my father would have packed his bags for seminary that very afternoon. But no—he fought it. He was in a musical group with his brothers at the time, and didn't want to leave home. More importantly, he was keen on a certain girl in town. Jesus would just have to wait.

My mother, Ada Jackson, was quite a looker in her day. (She still is, in a motherly sort of way.) She was elected Cotton Queen at the county fair, and my father first noticed her there in the parade. He wooed her with his guitar, crooning songs like "Let Me Call You Sweetheart."

When Mama first told me that story, I couldn't believe it. I never knew my father to play a guitar, much less sing anything other than hymns. What made him change? I didn't know—not till after Father's accident.

⁂

That Easter Sunday, I didn't catch a single fish. I'd never been skunked on a warm April day before—surely God was smiting me.

I waited till dusk before heading home, and made sure the lamp was burning in Father's study window before I crept inside and up the stairs to my room. I slipped under the covers without taking off my fishing clothes.

From the kitchen below, I could hear the tinkling of dishes as Mama washed them. The door to Father's study creaked open and slammed shut, and heavy footsteps made their way across the hall.

My parents always had their serious talks in the kitchen; they never suspected that I could hear every word. This night, there was no talking for a long while. Father huffed and groaned; Mama kept scrubbing. Finally, Father spoke. "Ada, what have we done to deserve this?"

Mama didn't answer. Father repeated his question, louder and more forcefully. "Where did we go wrong?"

Still no answer. But I could almost hear the sound of gears clanking in Father's head as he marshaled his arguments, preparing to strike.

"Ours is a Christian family," he began, his voice booming as though he were in church. "We do things different from the rest of the world. And one of the ways we honor God is by keeping the Sabbath. That's not just a suggestion—no, sir. It's one of God's great commandments."

As Father paused to reload, Mama sighed. "Tobias is almost twenty years old," she said. "It's time for him to make his own decisions."

"As long as the boy is under my roof he is under my discipline," Father shot back. "A child is like an unruly tree—in order to grow up straight, he must be pruned. 'Raise up a child in the way he should go, and he will not depart from it.'"

I knew I was in trouble whenever he started quoting Scripture.

"He's not a child," Mama said.

"Dishonoring the Sabbath is grave enough," Father continued. "But that's not my only concern. The boy has grown despondent—dull to the things of the Lord. He doesn't study the Scriptures. Why, the only thing he reads on Sunday is the funny papers. He fritters away his time on—"

"Tobias is a good boy," Mama said. "All he needs is a wife. When he starts a family of his own, he'll see—"

"And where will he find a Christian wife, if not in church? You suppose he'll find a suitable helpmate at the lake? "

An iron skillet clanged against the sink. "You didn't find *me* in church."

"And look what happened," Father said. "I was wrong."

"Wrong about what?"

"Wrong to look for a wife at a place of amusement instead of in the Lord's house. We've made do, Ada, and I've repented of my past. But—it wasn't God's will for me to marry you."

There was a long silence. Mama walked over to icebox and lifted out a chicken to thaw.

I suspect that Father regretted the words as soon as they were out of his mouth, but there was no going back now. And so he barreled forward, throwing out Bible verses like hand grenades. "Who is the head of this home? 'Wives, be ye subject to your husbands, for the husband is the head of the wife.' You've flaunted my authority, coddled that boy, and let him do as he pleases. 'A father that spareth the rod hateth his child.' I will not sit idly by while my son goes to hell in—"

I heard a great thud and then a crash, followed by the sound of a frozen chicken wobbling over the floor.

Father scrambled towards the door, pursued by shattering plates and cups. I froze to my bed, my heart pounding so hard I couldn't breathe.

Outside, the Plymouth roared to life. Father tore out of the drive, tires spitting gravel, while Mama yelled after him: "Go to hell, you damn-blasted son of a bitch!"

For having sworn only once before, Mama sure was good at it.

CHAPTER 2

FROM DOWNSTAIRS, I heard Mama sweeping up the broken dishes. I thought about going down to see if she was all right, but I couldn't bring myself to move.

I kept thinking over Father's words. He was right about my life being aimless; but what was there for me in Remus? All my friends had split town, jumping trains bound for Detroit or wherever else work might be found.

Though he never said it outright, I got the feeling that Father wanted me to follow in his footsteps and go to seminary. Becoming a preacher was the last thing I wanted to do, and no cow had kicked me upside the head to convince me otherwise.

What did I want out of life? Only one thing, really. To make love to a beautiful girl before the Rapture. Which didn't leave much time; according to Father, the End Times began the day they lifted Prohibition. Any minute now, Jesus was liable to come bursting out of the clouds on a white horse, sword in hand, ready to wreak some vengeance.

My worst fear was that I'd finally find a girl, we'd tie the knot, and *then*, on our wedding night—just when she was about to drop her dress—Jesus would come riding in on that infernal horse and whisk us up to heaven, where we'd be like angels and never get to have sex.

But there was no need to worry about that anymore, thanks to Lars Lundgren. Now the only girls left in town were clunkers like Hulda Thrune.

As far as occupations went, my secret ambition was to be a newspaper cartoonist. Every week, I'd go down to Bob's Barber Shop and salvage the old comic sections out of the wastebasket. *Mutt and Jeff, Krazy Kat, Bringing Up Father, The Katzenjammer Kids, Popeye*—I loved them all.

Father didn't approve. He held that the Bible was the only thing worth reading. Made-up stories were just that—lies. And newspapers were worthless. "If you really want to know what's happening in the world," he'd say, "read the Book of Revelation."

When I was a boy, Father would tuck me into bed and read to me every night. Other children got to hear a fairy tale or adventure story as they drifted off to sleep. I got Leviticus and Deuteronomy.

For all the Scripture I was subjected to, you'd think I would have known the whole Bible, frontwards and back. But, I came to find out, there were some parts of the Bible that Father never read.

One Sunday during church, when I was about twelve years old, I was sitting next to Eddie Quackenbush. In the middle of the sermon, Eddie poked me in the ribs and whispered, "Did you know that the Bible talks about Mrs. Pike?" (Mrs. Pike was our Sunday school teacher.) I tried to ignore him, but Eddie shoved his Bible under my nose and pointed to these words:

> We have a sister,
> and she hath no breasts.

My eyes about popped out of their sockets. I grabbed Eddie's Bible to see what book those words were in. *Song of Solomon*. Huh—twelve years of sermons and nightly Bible readings, and I'd never heard of *that* book.

Suddenly, I took an intense interest in Scripture study. That night, after Father finished with the usual selection from Ezra or Ezekiel and snuffed out the lamp, I lit a candle and opened my Bible to the Song of Solomon. I started at the first page, to see if this little book had any other interesting verses. God rewarded my curiosity.

> A bundle of myrrh is my beloved to me;
> he shall lie all night between my breasts.

For me, there was no greater revelation than finding breasts in the Bible. I'd have sooner expected to find beer at a Baptist picnic. And yet, the Song of Solomon was practically bursting with breasts!

> Thy stature is like to a palm tree,
> and thy breasts to clusters of grapes.
> I said, "I will go up to the palm tree;
> I will take hold of the boughs thereof."

Wherever I turned, there they were—swelling like ripe fruit, rising like towers, leaping like twin gazelles.

> Thy breasts are like two young fawns,
> twins of a gazelle, that frolic among the lilies.

I'd read some pretty racy stuff in *Cowboy Love Tales*, but no romance-writer that ever lived had anything on King Solomon.

I wrote down all the juiciest verses and stashed them in my secret lock-box—the rusty medicine chest I kept hidden in a hollow tree stump out back of our house. My other treasures consisted of a few half-smoked cigarettes and a dirty comic book called "Tillie the Typist After Hours."

A year or so later, I added the crowning gem to my collection. Nosing around the rail yards one afternoon, I found it in an old boxcar, probably left there by a tramp. It was a photograph of a real, live, naked lady, stretched out on a fancy couch with one arm up behind her head. She must have been French, because she had more hair under her arm than I did.

That picture awakened new longings in me—longings I didn't even know my body was ready for. And so, with visions of the French Lady in my head, I started rubbing myself between the legs and spilling my seed. I'd heard about this from other boys—jerking off, slapping the snake, choking the chicken, whacking the weasel. Now I knew what all the fuss was about.

I never dreamed of my true love, Emily Apple, when I did it. My intentions towards Emily were as pure as a saint's. But the French Lady was my mistress.

Mama kept a stack of women's medical books in her bottom dresser drawer, and sometimes I'd peek at them when my parents were out of the house. That's how I learned words like *ova, semen,* and *vulva*—along with more disturbing words like *vaginal discharge* and *menstruation.* One of these books warned about boys like me:

> Teach your boy that when he handles or excites the sexual organs, all parts of the body suffer. This is why it is called "self-abuse." The sin is terrible, and is, in fact, worse than lying or stealing. For, although these are wicked and will ruin the soul, self-abuse will ruin both soul and body. This loathsome habit lays the foundation for consumption, paralysis, and heart disease. It makes many boys lose their minds; others, when grown, commit suicide.

That put the fear of God in me. I tried my best to kick the loathsome habit; one Sunday during the altar call, I even stumbled down the aisle and blubbered the Sinner's Prayer. But admitting I was a sinner didn't kill the desire.

No matter how many times I asked Jesus into my heart, it wouldn't take.

The summer I turned 16, I tried getting baptized. Father said that the Old Man was gone now, drowned in the baptismal waters, and I was a new and spotless creation. That worked for about a month. Then the Old Man crept back under my skin and wrapped his bony fingers around my heart.

Whenever I did manage to put off the habit for a couple weeks, the French Lady would enter my dreams and I'd spill my seed in bed. I hated wet dreams—they startled me awake and created a mess. I was terrified that Mama would notice the stains on my sheets.

I wondered—did Jesus ever spill his seed? Being fully a man, I figured, his body must have produced semen in the usual amount. And it had to escape one way or the other, or his balls would have exploded. So did Jesus have wet dreams? What were they about?

These questions vexed me considerably. The Bible didn't give any answers, and I knew I couldn't ask Father. That would have exposed me for the unrepentant sinner I was. If I were truly redeemed, I wouldn't even think about such things.

Lying in bed that Easter night, waiting to hear the Plymouth pull back into the drive, I realized that Father was right. I *was* headed for hell.

I remembered a word Father had used in one of his sermons: *predestination.* A small number of people—the elect—are predestined to heaven from the start. And everybody else is predestined to hell, and there's nothing you can do about it. You know you're among the elect if you love to pray and read the Bible above all else. But if you love girls more than God, it's a sure bet you've got a one-way ticket south.

All these years I'd tried to hide my sins and blend in with God's elect, but it was clear now that I was among the damned. Because of me, my parents were on the brink of divorce, if not murder.

And so I resigned myself to hell. It wasn't a great disappointment, though. Heaven, Father said, was one long church service where the saints sang through the Baptist Hymnal again and again, into infinity. Eternal torment by Satan and his minions sounded rosy by comparison—especially if the French Lady was there with me.

CHAPTER 3

THE NEXT MORNING, I awoke to the sound of a car crunching up the drive. I rolled out of bed and stumbled over to the window. There was a large black auto in the driveway, but it wasn't Father's—it was a patrol car.

When I got downstairs, Officer Radney was already in the kitchen. There was no mistaking him; everyone in town knew Radney Larse, Remus's one and only lawman.

"This is the hardest part of my job, ma'am" he said, scanning the kitchen to avoid looking at Mama. "Yes siree."

Mama's face was flushed and her hands were trembling. "Malachi. Is—is he—?"

Officer Radney fixed his gaze on a basket of biscuits left over from the night before. "Do you mind?"

Mama was confused. "No, I—"

"Much obliged." He sauntered over and bit off a cheekful of biscuit. "Now. You were asking . . ."

"Malachi—"

"Ah, yes. The Reverend." Radney coughed, spraying crumbs through the air. "Well, he's seen better days, but he's still in one piece. Can't say the same for that Ford."

"It's a Plymouth," I said. "Brand new."

"Ain't no more." Officer Radney bowed his head for a moment. "I'll take you to the church—that's where it happened."

As Mama and I started towards the door, Radney pocketed two more biscuits.

It was a cold, gray morning. Sure enough, I thought, yesterday's balmy weather was only a fluke. Mama and I slid onto the hard leather seat in back of the patrol car.

"Lord have mercy," Mama said, over and over. Her prayers floated up in white clouds of warm breath and flattened into a layer of fog on the cold window.

Father had never much liked Officer Radney. During Prohibition, Radney turned a blind eye to the stills and speakeasies, giving Remus a reputation as "Michigan's Whiskey Woods." Father often had condemned Radney from the pulpit; this must have been sweet revenge.

It didn't take long to reach the church. "There she is," Radney said, turning up the drive. "What's left of her."

A pair of tire tracks spun off the drive and ate through the grass, leading to a gaping hole in the side of the church. The Plymouth's tail protruded forth. Loose parts were scattered over the ground—hubcaps, headlights, a door, the steering wheel. That car was the one luxury Father allowed himself; he justified it on account of a preacher needing a nice car to lead funeral processions.

"The Reverend got thrown from the vehicle before impact," Radney said. "I found him lyin' over there, passed out. Lucky thing there ain't parts of him spread all over, too." Radney laughed but Mama didn't.

He hopped out and opened the door. "Follow me— he's inside the church."

It was raining harder now. We stepped over shards of metal, glass, and wood, making our way to the church. At the door, Radney turned to face Mama. "I hate to be the one to tell you, ma'am," he said, "but the Reverend was inebriated."

Mama shot him a glare. "What?"

"Drunk."

"Not Malachi. Impossible—"

"As a skunk," Radney said. "Go on in and smell for yourself."

Father was hunched over in the back pew—the same seat where I sat most Sundays, doodling in my notebook and dodging the sermon. Mama tried to rouse him, but Father hid his face in his hands. I didn't see any blood, but on top of his head was a big purple goose-egg from the frozen chicken.

Radney sauntered up behind Mama and lit a cigarette. "One thing I forgot to tell you," he said. "There's something funny with his eyes. When I found him, there was white stuff splattered all over his face. I wiped it off, but he still couldn't see anything. Had to lead him in here like a blind man."

Mama fanned away the smoke. "What kind of white stuff?"

"At first I thought was paint—till I smelt it. It's the damndest thing but, while he was lying there, a bird must've flew over and, you know, shit on his face. Pardon the language." Radney cast a glance around the sanctuary. "Don't know what kind of bird could've dropped a load that size. Must've been a big mother."

I was too shocked to feel anything, but Mama started to cry.

Radney tried to put his hand on her shoulder, but she jerked away. After an awkward silence, he dropped his cigarette on the church floor and ground it out. "Got to get back to the station and file a report."

File a report, my ass. Radney drove straight to Bob's Barber Shop to gloat. By noon, the whole town was abuzz over Father's disgrace.

The church elders held an emergency meeting that night and declared Father unfit for ministry. They gave us two months to vacate the parsonage and find a new home. Brother Lester Crouch was appointed interim pastor.

Brother Lester and his wife had thirteen children whose names were all from the Bible and started with "J"—John, Josiah, Jerusha, Jehosephat, and so on. (I always wondered when they'd get stuck with Jezebel.) Lester was the obvious choice for pastor, I guess, since he'd sired half the congregation.

The next day, the *Remus Register* carried a front-page exposé. A fallen preacher was big news for a paper usually devoted to livestock trades, obituaries, and reports of unusually-shaped vegetables.

According to the *Register*, Father had driven to the Beaver Lodge, a tavern north of town. "He came in and sat alone in a corner," the tavern keeper said.

Nobody knew who he was. After about an hour, I told him to order up or get out. We don't stand for vagrants loitering around. Then he asked for apple juice. Now, nobody asks for apple juice this time of year unless they mean the hard stuff, so I brought him a mug of hard cider. He sure liked it, because he ordered up another mug, and then another. After eight or ten mugs, his spirits lightened considerably. Then he told us he was a preacher, so the boys asked him to lead in a hymn. He obliged with "Brighten the Corner Where You Are," and everybody joined him on the chorus:

> *Brighten the corner where you are!*
> *Someone far from harbor you may*
>   *lead across the bar,*
> *So brighten the corner where you are!*

Reverend Henry really raised the roof on that part about the bar. After that, he stood up on the pool table and preached a sermon about how Jesus turned water into liquor. By the end, he was whooping and hollering. It was a regular revival. A little while later, he slipped out the door. Drove off without even paying. I should have known better than to trust a preacher.

Mama and I could scarcely believe it. Father was such a strict teetotaler that he never even touched grapes; "wine in the cluster," he called them. But, as with Adam and Eve, apples were his undoing.

CHAPTER 4

FOR A FULL WEEK, Father didn't say a single word. He stayed in his study, taking only bread and water. Mama tried reading the Bible aloud to him, but he waved her away.

On the eighth day, I was sitting in the kitchen when Mama came to fetch me. "Your father wants to talk with you."

"What about?" I wondered if he blamed me for what happened. Maybe he'd been stewing all this time, getting ready to bawl me out.

"How should I know? All he said was 'Bring me Tobias.'"

"That's it?"

"He won't even talk to me. If he wasn't so pathetic, I'd give him another thrashing."

Usually when Father called me into his study, I'd stare out the window to evade his probing gaze. I was afraid that if I looked into his eyes, he'd see right through to my soul; he'd pry open my heart like my secret box and spread the contents out on his desk for examination.

But there was nothing to hide from this time. Father slouched in his chair with a black bandana tied over his eyes. For a long while, neither of us said anything. I was surprised at how old he looked; I hadn't noticed him going gray, but now his hair was more white than brown. And set against that black cloth, his skin was ghastly pale. He looked like a dead man alive.

Father must have sensed my sadness. "Tobias," he said. "Don't pity me. I am the Lord's clay pot, but I made myself a vessel of dishonor. He's returning me to the potter's grounds, grinding me back into the clay so that I can be made anew. This is my punishment, and the Lord is just."

"You'll preach again." I said. "There's lots of blind evangelists."

"But not drunk evangelists." Father tightened his grip on the chair's arms. "I will not ask for mercy. I don't deserve it. All I can hope for is that my life will serve as a warning to others."

"How can I help?"

"You can't help me. But your mother—" Father choked up. "Because of my sin, she will suffer. If I die penniless and starved, so be it. But I can't bear the thought of Ada—"

"I'll do anything," I said. "I'll get a job."

He shook his head. "There's no work in Remus."

"I'll go to Grand Rapids—or Detroit. Work in a factory."

"The car is gone. In seven weeks, we'll lose this house. I've been turning it over in my mind, and there's only one hope."

"What's that?"

Father put his hands together and touched his fingers to his lips as though he were praying. He seemed unsure of his idea—maybe he was afraid to say it because it was the only one he had.

"I need you to fetch a book," he said. "It's on the top shelf, behind my set of Jonathan Edwards."

I remembered Father quoting Jonathan Edwards once in a sermon: he said that the road to hell is paved with the skulls of unsaved babies. I hoped Father didn't want me to read something like that at a time like this.

"Pull down a couple volumes," he said, "and reach back behind. There should be a small book with a green cover."

"I think I can feel it . . . "

When I brought the book out into the light, I couldn't believe my eyes. It was a Western novel—*Comrades of the Saddle*.

So my father had secrets of his own.

I peeled open the cover and read the inscription: "To Malachi Henry, the Texas Troubador; with love, Ada Jackson, Christmas 1914."

"In the middle of that book," Father said, "you'll find a piece of paper."

I found the sheet, unfolded it, and spread it out on Father's desk. It was a broadside advertisement:

CHRISTMAS EVE DANCE
Town Hall, Glen Rose
Dec. 24, 1914
Music provided by
The Golden Melody Makers
Admission 50 cents

"You were in a music group?" I asked.

"My brothers and me, yes. Our sisters sang with us sometimes, but mostly it was Wilburn, JP, and me. The three of us used to set on the front porch every night after chores were done. Will played banjo and JP played the fiddle. My fingers couldn't move fast enough to pick a banjo or mandolin. All I could ever do was strum the guitar and sing."

"What sort of songs?"

"Oh, 'Yellow Rose of Texas,' 'Speckled Top Shoes,' 'Jack of Diamonds'—all the old ones."

Father leaned back in his chair, and his lips eased into the faint glimmer of a smile. "We were only playing for fun, but folks told us we should start up a band. So one day we up and did. Called ourselves the Golden Melody Makers. We played dance halls, roadhouses, fairs—all the way from Glen Rose to Fort Worth. We couldn't believe that folks would pay to hear us, but they did. Before long, I had a big pile of money stashed under my mattress. Will and JP blew theirs, but I saved mine. I didn't tell anybody about the money—not even Ada."

Father wasn't using his preacher's voice anymore. He was talking to me like a confidant, a friend.

"Why did you give it up?" I asked.

"Daddy got to where he couldn't work the farm anymore, and Will had to take over. I married your mama and went off to seminary. It was time to give up childish things.

"For a time, I thought I could keep playing on the side. But at seminary, I learned that God is glorified by spiritual hymns. Worldly music glorifies Satan. One of my teachers told me that I had to choose between my guitar and Jesus. He said, 'Would Jesus ever sing about women, or gambling, or drinking?' Those words convicted me, and I smashed my old guitar. I vowed to sing nothing but hymns for the rest of my life.

"But I didn't know what to do with all that money. I didn't know any better when I earned it, but it was surely tainted now. I decided to burn it, but I couldn't bring myself to go through with it. What if, someday, God wanted to give it away to help others? So I stuffed it all into a leather pouch and dropped it into an old, dry well on my family's farm. Then I threw in some dirt on top and boarded over the hole so no one would see it."

Father stopped and leaned in towards me. "Now take that piece of paper," he said, "and turn it over."

On the back of the advertisement, there were faint pencil markings.

"It's a map," Father said. "I drew it to mark where that well was, so I'd never forget."

It looked like a child's drawing—a wiggly line for a river, some trees, boxes for buildings. Looking at that map, I realized that Father had drawn it when he was my age.

His handwriting even looked like mine. For the first time, I realized that Father had once been a lot like me.

"I need you to go to Texas," he said. "To Glen Rose. To get that money."

"Texas?" That was impossible. I'd never traveled alone anywhere further than Grand Rapids—how could I find my way to Texas?

"This is all the money I've got," Father said, handing me a wad of moist bills. "How much is it?"

I counted. "Thirty-seven bucks."

"Good—that's enough to get you there. Take the evening flyer to Chicago. Then change over to the St. Louis line, and take it all the way down to Fort Worth."

"Tonight?"

"There's no time to lose. Don't let your mama catch wind of this, either. She wouldn't stand for me sending you out alone."

"What happens when I get to Fort Worth?"

"Pay someone to drive you to Glen Rose, then search out your Uncle Wilburn." Father thought for a moment. "Don't tell him what's happened to me."

He reached out and I took his hand. Father pulled me close and gave me a quick hug. "Godspeed, son. May an angel of the Lord watch over you."

I left the room in a daze, wondering if this was all

real—or if I'd finally gone insane from whacking the weasel.

Somewhere inside my father, the boy Malachi—who loved gunslingers, guitars, and girls—was still there. He was buried as deep as a treasure in a dry well, but he was still breathing. Otherwise, Father would have burned that cowboy novel years ago.

If I brought back the money, could I help Father resurrect his boyish soul? Or was one quest as foolish as the other?

CHAPTER 5

I PULLED OUT OF REMUS at midnight, with nothing in my pack but Father's money and map, a change of clothes, and some dried venison for snacking. By the time we reached Grand Rapids, I'd eaten all the deer jerky and my mouth was on fire.

At the station, I gulped down some water and bought a ticket for the Chicago line. "You'll want a bed," the agent told me. "You can't get any sleep sitting up in coach. I'll give you a berth with a window, too." I figured a good night's sleep was worth the extra expense.

The porter stowed my pack and showed me to my compartment. I climbed the ladder and rolled onto a paper-thin mattress. When I stretched out, my feet slid off the end and pressed against the cold shell of the train. Overhead, there was about one inch of air between my nose and the roof.

I scooted onto my side and, with some effort, found the narrow opening the ticket man had called a window. Once I clicked off the light, I was able to see the stars; it felt like my bed had left earth and was now floating through the night sky. Each click-clack of the rails carried me further from the only world I'd ever known. My life seemed like a speck of dust in comparison to the universe.

Pondering my own insignificance, I drifted off to sleep. Then the wheels banged across a loose rail joint and slammed my forehead against the roof.

After the throbbing subsided, my eyes fluttered back shut. In my half-sleep, I imagined that the train berth was a coffin. I was being buried alive. I pushed against the roof but it wouldn't budge. I tried to yell but no sound would come out of my mouth. I jolted awake, slammed my head against the roof again, and slowly came back to my senses.

I became aware of a nagging tingle in my loins. The water I'd drunk in Grand Rapids had made its way through my system and was itching to get out. Damn— there was no chance of sleeping now. No way in hell was

I going to leave my berth in search of a john. If there's anything worse than a Michigan outhouse, it's a Michigan outhouse on wheels. I pinched together my legs and stared out the window.

After an hour or so, the starry night faded into a gray haze. The sun made a faint yellow stain on the horizon. Then I saw the first signs of Chicago—shanty houses, church steeples and smokestacks, workers huddled on train platforms. We rumbled on between rows of brick houses the color of rotten teeth.

As we hurtled into the heart of the city, the wheels screeched and the engine lurched. I gripped the sides of my mattress and braced my feet against the end of the car, fearing that my bladder would explode on impact. Finally, the beast ground to a halt and bellowed out a dying wheeze.

I jumped out of my berth like Lazarus out of hades, with an urgent need to piss.

In Chicago Union Station, groggy passengers poured out onto the platform. I'd never seen so many people—a teeming sea of black overcoats, suits, and dresses. I rode the current down several flights of stairs and into a great hall, all the while humming a tune:

Chicago, Chicago, that toddlin' town;
Chicago, Chicago, I'll show you around.
Bet your bottom dollar you'll lose the blues in Chicago,
Chicago, the town that Billy Sunday couldn't shut down.

I'd been to Chicago once before, when I was about ten. Father took me to see Billy Sunday preach a revival. It was under a circus tent packed with sinners, and all I remember is that right in the middle of his sermon, Billy picked up a chair over his head and then threw it down, smashing it to splinters. Billy stared out over the crowd with wild eyes. "Did I scare the devil out of you? Well that's what I'm a tryin' to do!" I wet my pants.

That was the third or fourth time I got saved. Whenever I feared I was in imminent danger of death, I'd call on Jesus and beg for salvation. The rest of the time, I didn't give him any thought. Jesus was like an insurance policy against eternal fire.

Father came home from that trip converted, too. From then on, he wanted to be the Billy Sunday of Remus. The next week during his sermon, he even tried throwing a chair. It knocked over the pulpit, and sent the Bible flying—but the chair remained unscratched. I don't recall whether anybody got saved, but three old ladies wet *their* pants. Billy Sunday couldn't shut down Chicago. My father couldn't even shut down Remus.

Now, I was in danger of wetting my pants in Chicago for the second time. It wasn't easy finding a john in Union Station. The great hall looked like something out of ancient Babylon, with its marble columns and vaulted ceiling.

That got me thinking about Samson, and how he was kept prisoner in a hall just like this. After Delilah cuts off his hair, Samson is captured by the Philistines. They forgot about him for a while but, during a big party, they bring him out for laughs and chain him between two pillars. But his hair has grown back just enough that he's able to pull down the pillars, squashing everybody in the place. The story of Samson always was my favorite Bible tale. A man of super strength, the seductress who betrays him, the mass carnage—it's better than an Errol Flynn movie.

I was standing in the middle of Chicago Union Station imagining Samson pulling the whole place down, when someone bumped into me. "Watch it, rube!"

Then somebody else knocked my pack off my shoulder. "Keep it moving, hayseed."

Onlookers chimed in. "Whaddaya think this is, a cornfield?"

I was wearing a canvas jacket and my best shirt—red plaid with pearl buttons. Fancy duds by Remus standards, but I stuck out like a sore thumb in Chicago. The crowd pushed me through the hall and swept me out into the street. I stood on the corner trying to get my bearings amidst the shouting pedestrians and honking cars.

"Hey kid—never seen a crossing signal?"

More laughter. "Where he's from, they've only got cattle crossings."

I walked along the sidewalk till I came to a staircase leading underground. The smell of stale urine wafted up from below. Finally, I thought—a john. I ventured forth into the dark, damp corridor.

Halfway down the stairs, I bumped into something: the saggy ass of a disheveled old man. The man had his pants down around his ankles and was he peeing right there on the stairs.

He looked as startled as me. "It's all right brother, I'm almost done." Polite though he was, I turned and ran.

Hell, I thought—they must not have johns in Chicago. So I found a dark alley of my own and did my business.

CHAPTER 6

I'D THOUGHT THAT NO PLACE could be more boring than northern Michigan—that is, until I crossed the godforsaken Land of Lincoln. The whole state seemed to be one empty field, as long and plain as Honest Abe himself.

To pass the time, I read a travel magazine. Only one item held my interest—an advertisement for Fred Harvey's restaurant at St. Louis Union Station. It wasn't the food that whet my appetite, though. "Featuring the world-renowned Harvey Girls, the Acme of Femininity, beautiful in Form and Spirit, individually hand-picked by Mr. Harvey for exceptional Composure and Grace."

After reading that description, I wanted to hand-pick one myself.

At Bloomington Station, an old man boarded the train. There were empty seats all around, but he sat right next to me. His white linen suit reeked of mothballs. I stuffed the Harvey Girls brochure into my pocket and went back to counting silos.

A few miles out, the old man stood up and paced the aisle, staring into people's faces. The porter asked if he was looking for something, but he just grunted. When the porter left the car, the old man made his way up front and pulled a small leather Testament—just like my father's travel Bible—out of his inside pocket. No one else seemed to notice, but my heart was pounding.

"Ladies and gentlemen," he said, "I want you all to know that I've found the Lord."

For a moment, an awful silence weighed in the air. Then somebody yelled from the back of the car. "Found him? When did he get lost?"

Everyone laughed except the evangelist—and me. I sunk down in my seat, wishing to God he'd sit back down. But he continued undaunted, as evangelists always do.

"The day of judgment is nigh. Soon, you will be called to account for your wicked deeds. Brothers and sisters, let me ask you this: are you prepared to die?"

Another passenger groaned. "I ain't yer brother. Siddown for Chrissakes."

The evangelist flinched like he'd been slapped. He gripped his Testament with both hands. "Thou shalt not take the name of thy God in vain. That's the Second Commandment. Satan is stoking his fires for the likes of you, sinner friend." The veins on his neck and forehead bulged. "Turn to the Lord while there's still time! Fall before his throne and plead for mercy!"

Tall and gaunt, he looked like a stretched-out, funhouse-mirror image of my father. Maybe that's why I felt sorry for him. I wanted to pull him aside and tell him that this sort of talk may get you an "amen" at Remus Baptist, but it will only get you rotten tomatoes from a train full of Chicagoans.

The evangelist lowered his voice to a whisper. "Listen friends, I'm here to help you. To *warn* you. Your children are being lied to—led like innocent sheep to the slaughter. Let me ask you this: does anyone here really believe that his ancestor was a monkey?"

A shout from the back—"*Yours* was."

The passengers broke out laughing again. It was sport for them but torture for me. As ridiculous as the evangelist was, he was one of my people.

"Friends," he said. "This is not a laughing matter.

Tarry not, O sinners. The angel of death might claim your soul this very hour." I made the mistake of looking the evangelist in the face, and he locked his eyes on me. "*You there*. Have you settled your account with your maker? If this train were to fall off these tracks, would your soul to his bosom fly?"

At that moment, a crash like thunder shook the train. We jolted forward in our seats and the evangelist tumbled backwards, head over heels. A woman screamed. *We're all going to die*, I thought. *And me without ever getting to make love—or even getting to see a real live naked girl. I'd settle for that. But no—*

"Take me, Lord!" the evangelist cried. "I'm ready to go home!"

The brakes shrieked like a band of demons, sending a shower of red sparks past the windows. An awful smell—like burning rubber—filled the car. When the train finally ground to a halt, we all looked at each other in shocked silence. *Was the evangelist right? Had we arrived in hell?*

The back door slid open and the porter poked in his head. "Everyone all right in here? There's some cattle on the tracks. Nothing to worry about—we'll have 'em cleared off in no time."

Everyone breathed a sigh of relief and went back to

chattering and crinkling their newspapers. The evangelist brushed off his suit and slunk back to his seat, disappointed that this sinful old world was still spinning.

※※※

Thankfully, the evangelist got up to leave at the next stop. After the doors closed, I saw he'd left his Bible behind. Had he forgotten it, or left on purpose? Was his faith shaken, or was it meant to be a lifeline for my damned soul?

The little brown Bible lay right in the middle of his seat, looking like a sacred dropping from a man who ate, drank, and shat Scripture.

I wanted to let it smolder there, but I was afraid people might think that it was my Bible and I was a preacher, too. So I picked it up and buried it in a travel magazine.

Growing up, the Bible was as much a part of life as the air I breathed. There were no atheists in Remus—only believers and backsliders. I knew there were folks out there in the wide world who denied the Scriptures, but I'd never met any. Now, here I was in a car full of heathens, embarrassed even to be seen with the Good Book.

A few miles down the track, I cracked open the musty book—careful to keep it inside the magazine—and leafed

through its yellowed pages. I was used to hiding magazines inside my Bible so I'd have something to read during Father's sermons. I never would have dreamed that
someday I'd be doing it the other way around. But the
wasteland of Illinois had driven me to Scripture reading.
It wasn't just out of boredom, though; witnessing the
evangelist's humiliation ripped the bandage off my old
doubts.

I wanted to believe the Bible. But every time I tried
to read it, I got confused. It wasn't that I got lost halfway
through, either—my troubles started on the first page.
In Genesis 1, it says that God created the plants first, then
the animals, and people last. But in Genesis 2, it says that
God created Adam first, then the plants, then the animals,
and Eve last. Which was it? Not even God can have it
both ways.

Then comes the talking snake and the angel with the
flaming sword. Actually, the idea of a talking snake didn't
stretch my imagination too much. But after Adam and
Eve get kicked out of the Garden of Eden, God posts an
angel with a flaming sword at the garden gate to make
sure nobody ever tries moving back in. That means that
the Garden—and the angel with the flaming sword—are
still there today, somewhere on the banks of the Euphrates.
What if someone sent an army to conquer Eden? Sure,

an angel with a flaming sword can hold off Arab raiders on camelback—but how about a fleet of tanks?

Then there's Cain's wife. At the start of Genesis 4, Eve gives birth to two sons, Cain and Abel. After he kills Abel, Cain goes off and finds himself a wife. Cain and his wife have children of their own, then grandchildren, then great-grandchildren, then great-great grandchildren. And then—and only then—Adam and Eve, who are still alive and kicking, give birth to their third child. So if Adam and Eve are the parents of the whole human race, where did Cain's wife come from?

After that, there's a lot of begetting—which gets rather dull, even if it does involve sex. My interest perked up again with Genesis 6, where the beautiful girls come in. The girls are so beautiful, in fact, that angels swoop down from heaven and knock them up. Then the girls give birth to a race of giants. This story didn't seem entirely implausible to me: if I was stuck in heaven all day, I sure as heck would have flown down to get a closer look at Emily Apple.

Right after the giants are born, God gets mad at everybody and decides to destroy the whole world and start over. He takes Noah, the one righteous man on earth, and tells him to build a boat big enough to hold his family and two of every sort of animal. Every sort of animal, that is, except dinosaurs. Why didn't Noah save the dinosaurs, if God told him to bring two of *every* creature?

My father believed that dinosaurs weren't on the ark because they never really existed. It was all a hoax to lure people away from Scripture. The time he took me to Chicago, we visited the Field Museum and saw the Brontosaurus and Tyrannosaurus skeletons. My eyes were wide with wonder, but Father just chuckled. "Those Godless evolutionists glue a pile of chicken bones together and fool everybody. Well they can't fool Malachi Henry. *Chickensaurs*, that's what they are." Awfully big chickens, I thought.

Fresh off the ark, Noah throws a party where he gets punch drunk and strips off his clothes. When his youngest son, Ham, sees Noah's wrinkled old pecker, Noah curses Ham and his children forever. And this is the one righteous man on earth?

After that, there's more begetting—Noah's family has to get busy to repopulate the earth—and then things get dull again. A few chapters later, Abraham shows up. Abraham is an old man with a barren wife, and he wants nothing more than children. So God cuts a deal with him: God will give Abraham more children than he can count—if Abraham agrees to circumcise himself.

I first heard the word *circumcision* in Sunday school, the morning Eddie Quackenbush raised his hand and said, "Mrs. Pike, I was trying to read my Scriptures last night before bed, but there's one word that's got me puzzled and I can't figure out what it means."

Old Lady Pike's face lit up—Eddie was the last child on earth you'd expect to read the Bible on his own volition. "I'm so glad you asked, Edward. Now which word is that?"

"Circumcision."

Eddie never got an answer, because the old hag turned purple and ran out of the room.

Later, I asked my father what it meant. "It's the removal of the foreskin of the penis," he said.

It took me a minute to get over the shock of Father saying the word *penis*. "Re—removing? As in, cut—cut—cutting off?"

"That's right. With a knife."

I looked down at my crotch. "Did—did I have that done to me?"

He frowned. "Of course. It's a sign that your body is consecrated to God, every member of it."

The blood drained from my face. And from my injured member, too. From that day on, I was haunted by the ghost of my foreskin. What did it look like? Would girls like me better if I still had one? Did chopping it off stunt my growth? Was that why I still hadn't hit puberty?

After Abraham gives his 99-year-old pecker a shave, the lowly foreskin becomes a major player in the Bible. It becomes the defining mark of God's chosen people. Things really get crazy in the Book of Samuel, when David slaughters 200 Philistines, circumcises their corpses, and brings the bloody foreskins to King Saul on a silver platter—in exchange for the king's daughter. And this was the same David who killed Goliath? Every Baptist boy's hero? Author of the Book of Psalms?

My life would be a lot less confusing, I thought, if only God had told Abraham to cut the whole damn thing off.

The idea that we evolved from monkeys was tough to swallow. But what was the alternative? Flaming swords, fornicating angels, faked dinosaurs, and Philistine foreskins? No wonder the Chicagoans heckled that old evangelist.

As far as I could see, there were only two possibilities. Either the evangelist was right—and my father with him—or the Chicagoans were right.

If the evangelist was right, this life was nothing more

than a waiting room for the next. The only thing on earth that mattered was placing your reservation for eternity. And, considering how I preferred the French Lady over Jesus, I'd already bought my ticket to that warm place down South.

But if the Chicagoans were right, there was no hell—and no heaven, either. This life was all there is. You're born, you eat, you shit, you fuck, you die.

Funny thing was, the Chicagoans seemed happy, while the evangelist—sure of his eternal reward—didn't. Then I realized why: if no one's keeping score, there are no rules. If there is no Judgment Day, you can do whatever you want. Forget about laws and obligations—follow your whims and enjoy life while it lasts.

As we pulled into St. Louis, the last ember of my childhood faith flew out the window and disappeared in a stream of smoke. For the first time in my life, I was free to do whatever I wanted.

Bring on the Harvey Girls.

CHAPTER 7

FRED HARVEY'S RESTAURANT was right inside the station, so all I had to do was follow the scent of succulent flesh. My belly was as famished for food as my eyes were for pretty girls.

A man in a tuxedo showed me to a table in back, where I scanned the menu and the room. Once I got my bearings, I couldn't believe my eyes. *Those* were the Harvey Girls? Beautiful in form and spirit?

What a crock. They looked like a bunch of damn Pilgrims in a Thanksgiving Day pageant, with their starched white collars and black dresses that touched the floor. You couldn't even see their forms. Aside from their hands and faces, you wouldn't know they had bodies at all.

My waitress looked and talked like a prissy school marm. I always figured I was damned to wind up with a girl like that—mousy, pious, with thin lips, pencil-drawn eyebrows, and granny glasses. That was the only sort of girl who'd ever want to marry a preacher's boy. She wouldn't give me so much as a kiss before we were married. And after we got hitched, she'd undress in the dark so I'd never get to see her naked.

The acme of femininity? Those Harvey Girls were straight out of my worst nightmares. I chowed down my hamburger and got the hell out of there.

Unlike Chicago Union Station, they had bathrooms in St. Louis. In fact, they had two different kinds: White and Colored. It took me a minute to figure out that *Colored* didn't mean red and blue toilets. In Remus, nobody was scared to use the same john as a black man. I knew from experience: white shit doesn't look any different from colored.

Remus had quite a few Negroes, known as the Old Settlers. Nobody knew how they got there—maybe the Underground Railroad—but they'd been there as long as anyone could remember. My best friend at school, Sammy Swisher, was one of them.

Walking to school together one winter morning, Sammy and I found a dead skunk, frozen stiff. The whole rest of the way, we played skunk hockey, kicking it back and forth over the ice. When we got to school, there was a note on the door: no class—Mrs. Steinke was home sick. That gave Sammy an idea.

We went inside and propped the skunk up in her chair. I found a pair of Mrs. Steinke's wire glasses in the desk drawer, and set them on its nose. To top it all off—Sammy wrote "Mrs. Stinky" in huge letters across the blackboard.

Mrs. Steinke never lived it down. Neither did she ever catch the culprits. She suspected Sammy, but he had a perfect alibi: he'd been with the preacher's son all day.

❧❧❧

My experiment in doing whatever I wanted was off to a poor start, but the possibilities before me were endless. First thing, I left the station and walked until I came to the Fox Theater. When I saw the sign out front, I couldn't believe my luck: *Modern Times* was playing—Charlie Chaplin's new movie.

In Remus, the "theater" was a converted storage room in Bob's Barber Shop, with a wobbly projector in back and a white sheet up front. The film reels were old and grainy, with no sound other than old Bob's coughing and wheezing. I didn't mind too much, though—for a penny I could see Chaplin in *The Circus*, or Buster Keaton's *Sherlock Junior*, or Harold Lloyd's *Safety Last*.

Inside, the Fox didn't look like a theater at all. It was more like a temple to the God of Cinema. Everything was decked out in red and gold; satyrs and nymphs cavorted along the walls, and Oriental warriors stood watch from their pedestals high above. The ceiling of the auditorium was as wide as the night sky, painted deep blue with blinking lights for stars, with a chandelier as big as the moon in the center.

My favorite part of the movie was when they hooked Charlie up to the Billows Feeding Machine—"A practical device to feed your men while they work." The machine short circuits and dumps hot soup down Charlie's shirt, splats a pie in his face, shoves a metal bolt in his mouth, and slaps him silly with a sponge.

My other favorite part was Charlie's sidekick, played by Paulette Goddard. The title card called her "The Gamin, a child of the waterfront." Long, graceful legs, black hair wet with sea mist, strong cheekbones, cunning eyes, a tight-fitting dress torn at the bottom . . . For a child, Paulette Goddard sure was well-developed.

It was past 8 o'clock when the show let out, though you wouldn't have known for all the city lights. After the train ride, dinner, and food, I still had $29 and some change. A ticket to Fort Worth would only cost $10. That left me plenty of money to burn, and I had the urge to burn it. No more train berths for me. Tonight, I'd sleep in luxury.

And tomorrow——? I didn't know what I wanted to do next. Why go to Texas at all? Why did I owe it to my father? He brought this mess upon himself. Maybe I'd stay in St. Louis and get a job. Or head out to California, where I could pick oranges and sleep under the stars. But there was free money to be had in Texas. Maybe I'd get the money first, *then* go to California. I'd live like a king, sleeping in swanky hotels every night.

It was all too much to think about now. I could barely keep my eyes open. The first order of business was finding a place to sleep for the night.

I walked over to a hot dog stand. The proprietor was a red-haired, pimple-faced boy about my age, and I figured he'd know this town as well as anybody. "Excuse me," I said. "I'm not from around here and, well, what I'm wondering is——what's the best place to bed down around here?"

I always get nervous asking for help, so I was relieved when he gave me a friendly smile. "Out for a good lay tonight, eh pal?"

"That's right, someplace nice. Not a seedy flop-house—I mean someplace ritzy."

"I know just the place," he said. "Follow Grand to Market and hang right. Keep on for a couple blocks till you come to a pink house. Pink and purple, really big. You can't miss it."

"What's it called?"

"The Palace."

"You're sure it's nice?"

"The swankiest joint in town, pal. I can vouch for that myself. All the Harvey Girls stay there."

It sounded too bizarre to be true. Then again—if they showed movies in a Hindu temple, why wouldn't they sleep in a pink palace? I wanted to stay far away from those Harvey Girls, but it wasn't like I'd be in the same room with one. I tossed the pimple-faced boy a penny for his help and headed up Grand Avenue.

I'd never stayed in a hotel before, so I wasn't sure what to expect. Remus had only one hotel—the Remus Inn. It wasn't really an inn, though, just two spare rooms above Bob's Barber Shop. Bob Rufus—"Blind Bob," everyone called him—presided over a vast conglomeration of enterprises. His two-story brick building served as barbershop, movie theater, inn, and meeting hall. Bob wasn't truly blind, but he kept a bottle under the counter and would sneak a few nips in-between customers, which produced a similar effect. His barber business dried up for a while after he sliced off the top of Albert Denslow's ear—and that's when he cleared out two spare rooms and opened the inn. The inn turned out to be a bust, since nobody travels through Remus except the occasional northbound hunter. But if fleas and rats were paying customers, Bob would've been the richest man in town.

I hiked down Market Street for at least five blocks with no pink palace in sight. I began to have my doubts; but even if the boy was fooling with me, I figured, some other place was bound to turn up. The district was teeming with people, mostly colored. Doors opened and closed, spilling laughter and music out onto the street. Black men in white undershirts leaned against lamp poles, puffing on cigarettes and whistling at women. Old ladies leaned out of apartment windows and shouted gossip at each other. Street vendors hawked their wares. All this excitement, and I could barely keep my eyes open.

I trudged on, past bars and clubs and cabarets with dancing girls and blaring horns. More than anything, I wanted to go inside, order a drink, and take a load off, but

I didn't have the courage. I wasn't even sure if white folks were allowed.

Then, passing by an open door, I heard a sound that stopped me in my tracks. There was no wild laughter, no raucous music here. All was quiet except for a tinkling piano and a woman's voice.

> *Love for sale;*
> *Appetizing young love for sale;*
> *Love that's fresh and still unspoiled,*
> *Love that's only slightly soiled;*
> *Love for sale.*

I leaned against the window and let her voice wash over me. Through the glass and smoke, I glimpsed the singer, a black woman in a silver dress. She seemed to gather up all the sadness in the world, boil it down to its essence, and pour it out in her song.

> *Let the poets pipe of love*
> *In their childish way;*
> *I know every type of love*
> *Better far than they.*

Something tugged at my shoulder. I started to turn around and, behind me, a man had his arm halfway inside my pack. I yelled, pushed him away, and ran as fast as I could.

I ran till there were no more lights, no clubs, no crowds. When I stopped and looked back, I was the only soul on the sidewalk. That damn pimple-faced boy must have sent me down the one street in town that *didn't* have a hotel. My feet were sore and blistered. I sat down on a patch of grass and cursed everything and everyone who'd got me in this fix.

All the houses were dark except one—a Victorian mansion across the street. It was at least three stories high, a jumble of gables and dormers and wraparound porches, with a round turret off to one side. The lamps in the windows cast a red glow over the place, more eerie than inviting.

Red glow? *Couldn't be.* I got up to take a closer look. The hedges out front hadn't been trimmed in ages, and vines were crawling all over the verandah and up the walls. But yes, the siding was pink—with purple trim! I took back all my curses and thanked the pimple-faced boy a thousand times over.

Beside the door was a sign half-covered by ivy:

Le Palais
Cuisine Française

Cuisine—didn't that mean food? It was a damn restaurant, not a hotel. I started back to cursing.

It looked open, though, and I could hear voices inside. Maybe someone here could point me in the right direction. I rang the doorbell but no one answered, so I tried the door. It fell open, setting off a series of chimes. Inside the parlor, some gents were playing cards and snacking on what must have been some French *hors d'oeuvres*. Two ladies descended stairs, wearing silk gowns with necklines that plunged clear to their belly buttons. But it wasn't their belly buttons I noticed as they brushed past me.

From behind, a stern voice broke my reverie. "*Excuse me.*"

I turned to find a wide woman behind a narrow desk. "Pardon me, ma'am, I'm, uh—"

"*Mademoiselle,*" she said. "Mademoiselle Colette." Her face was ghastly white, with bright red lips and two slashes for eyebrows. A great mound of thick, blonde curls perched on top of her head.

"I'm sorry, Miss Colette. If you please, I—I seem to be lost."

"How may I be of assistance, monsieur?"

"I've come a long way, and I was looking to bed down for the night. So I asked where a nice place was, and—"

She raised a hand to silence me. "I'm sure you'll find

our accommodations quite satisfactory, monsieur."

I breathed easy and dropped my pack on the floor. Of course, I realized—all swanky hotels have restaurants on the first floor. At that moment, I could have kissed the mademoiselle. Hell, I could have kissed the pimple-faced boy. "You can't imagine how much this means to me."

Her mouth twisted into a smile. "Is this your first time?"

"First time anywhere. I'm from Remus, in Michigan, and back home we don't even have—"

"There's no need to explain," she said. "You look like a sweet one. I'll give you a discount—only seven dollars for the whole night." As I counted out my bills, she scanned her ledger. "What's your favorite month of the year—April, May, or June?"

"October, actually," I said. "I like the way the leaves—"

She snapped her ledger shut and handed me a key. "I think you'll like June."

CHAPTER 8

BY THE TIME I REACHED THE TOP of the stairs, I didn't give a damn about luxury anymore—I was ready to sleep in the hallway. But I staggered on like a drunkard till I found my room number. I rattled the key in the door, kicked it open, flung my pack on the floor, threw off my coat, yawned, and—without even turning on the light—lunged for the bed.

The bed was not as soft as I expected. In fact, it felt like there was something hard under the blankets. And that something seemed to be *moving*. Then it cursed. "Get the hell off me, you filthy bastard!"

Fingers clawed at my face and knees kicked at my groin. I tumbled off the bed, knocked over a lamp , and got tangled in the electrical cord. "I'm so sorry," I pleaded from the floor. "I thought this was my room—number eight—the number on the—"

"What do you think I am, a trampoline?"

"Why no—that is—let me—"

I propped the lamp back up, extracted my legs from the cord, and tried to get a handle on the situation. Either I had the wrong room, or this girl had the wrong bed.

One thing was certain—she wasn't happy about it. "I keep saying—no more drunks. And what does she send up? Some shit-faced punk . . . "

When I fixed the shade back on the lamp, she leaned over and clicked it on. The girl looked younger than she sounded—maybe sixteen or seventeen—with a powdered round face, bright red lips, blonde curls, and dark Theda Bara eyes. Her shoulders were bare, and she was wearing nothing but a sheet below them.

I backed up against the door and felt for the handle.

She looked me up and down. "My, you're a young one. I think I'll call you babyface."

She was calling *me* young? I gripped the doorknob, ready to run.

She straightened out the blankets and pillows around

her. "Well, aren't you going to sit down?"

I was confused—if this was her room, why did she want me to stay? And if it was my room, why didn't she get out?

"Don't stand there looking stupid, babyface."

I eased over to a wingback chair in the corner, ready to sort things out. "The lady downstairs told me room eight," I started.

The girl frowned and slapped the edge of the bed. "Over *here*, silly." That's when it dawned on me where I was—and what she was.

Temptress. Harlot. Whore. The words I'd heard in a thousand sermons echoed in my head. This was the sort of girl Father had always warned me about.

She didn't look particularly loose or fallen, whatever that meant. She was kind of cute, actually. I sat on the far end of the bed, with my back to her, then twisted around sideways.

She laughed. "Shy, are we? What's your name, babyface?"

I wondered whether I should make something up, but I was too tired to get creative. "Tobias. Tobias Henry."

She scooted up against the headboard, a sheet still covering her chest. "Tobias . . . that sounds like something out of the Bible."

My face turned red. "No. There's no Tobias in the Bible."

She snapped her fingers. "I got it—you're another one from the Bible college, ain't you?"

"I don't read the Bible." My mouth twitched. "I don't even believe in God." The evangelist's Bible was still in my pack, crying out against me.

Desperate to change the subject, I asked the first question that came to mind. "Say, are you a Harvey girl?"

She crossed her arms. "What's that supposed to mean?"

"I don't know. I just thought—"

"No, I'm a fucking Sister of Charity," she said. This girl could out-cuss my Mama.

I asked the next thing that came to mind. "Are you French?"

"Look, babyface. I don't get paid to answer stupid questions." With that, she hurled a pillow. I ducked and it glanced off my shoulder.

When I looked at her again, the sheet was down around her waist and her breasts were there right in the open, dangling like golden apples. My mouth fell open. I could only bear to look for a second, then I took a sudden interest in the wallpaper pattern.

"What's the matter?" she asked. "You look like

you've never seen a girl before."

I hadn't. Well, aside from one photograph, some cartoon drawings, and a hundred-thousand fantasies. But none of that prepared me for the real thing.

This was an unexpected opportunity. My goal had always been to get married and make love to a beautiful girl before the Rapture. But if there wasn't going to be any Rapture, and no Judgment, why wait?

I needed some time to think it all over. Finally, I said, "Do you mind if we just talked for a while?"

"*Talk?* I've *been* talking, babyface. What do you want to talk about?"

Well, it would be nice to talk about sex, for one thing. I'd never had a chance to talk to anyone about it before. For all the time I spent thinking about girls, I didn't know the first thing about what to do with them. All I knew about making love I'd learned from dirty comics and Mama's health books. The comics didn't offer much practical guidance; and those health books scared the dickens out of me, with their diagrams of female genitalia that resembled giant, man-eating tarantulas.

"Well," she said, "what are you waiting for? Afraid I'll bite?"

Maybe she would. I thought about that tarantula lurking under the sheet.

She looked at the clock on the wall. "Look, babyface, I ain't got all night. Let's get this over with."

"I paid for the whole night," I said. "The lady gave me a special."

"Damn it all," she said. "That's money out of *my* pocket. You'd better be a big tipper."

I thought she was talking about penis size. Did girls like them big? The thought terrified me. I'd never taken my shirt off in front of a girl, much less my shorts.

"What's wrong—can't get it up?"

That was the least of my problems—I was stiff as a flagpole. Finally, I decided to shut off my brain and let *that* part of me do the thinking. I climbed up onto the bed, and when I got close enough she grabbed my shirt and pulled me down onto her. Her breath was hot on my neck and her breasts were warm and soft against my chest, like bread dough. "Let's see what you're made of, babyface."

I sat up, straddling her waist, and tried to unbutton my pants with trembling fingers. The room seemed to be spinning around me. My head was swimming. Everything went blurry. I closed my eyes and tried to steady myself.

When I opened my eyes again, the girl's nipples were staring back at me like a pair of red eyes. And that's when I saw the bruise. Just below her breasts, on her left rib, there was a brown and purple blotch with veins spidering out. That wasn't the sort of tarantula I was expecting.

Who had hurt her—the big lady downstairs? Some Chicago businessman? My flagpole went limp as a noodle.

"Listen," I said, climbing off of her. "I—I'm too tired to do anything. I just came here looking for a place to sleep. You're a beautiful girl and all, but—"

"If you want me to suck you off—"

"No—that's not it. Really, I'm tired. So I'm going to take the floor and you can have the bed to yourself."

For the first time, she didn't say anything. I flattened out a blanket that had fallen off the bed and picked up the pillow she'd thrown. I curled up and listened to her breathing up above. It sounded like she was sniffling.

Why should I care? Why couldn't I just have my way with her? For whatever reason, I couldn't do it. I'd rather jerk myself off than pay a girl to pretend like she loved me.

I started thinking about Charlie Chaplin—how he rescued the Gamin, and how the two of them found a shack by the railroad tracks and made it a home. I imagined running away with the girl. We could find a cabin somewhere in the Ozarks. We could grow a garden and raise chickens.

Raising chickens with the girl sounded more appealing than screwing her—? What kind of fool notion was that? I knew less about raising chickens than I did about sex, if such a thing was possible.

Finally, I screwed up the courage to ask. "Have you ever thought about marriage?"

She let out a sharp laugh. "I told you—I don't answer stupid questions."

"I'll bet there's lots of fellows that want to marry you."

Another pillow came sailing over the edge of the bed, hitting me in the face. "Go to sleep. I don't talk to drunks."

The pillow was damp with tears.

CHAPTER 9

I WOKE UP THINKING OF HOSEA. That's the curse of being a preacher's son—you wake up in the same room with a naked girl for the first time in your life, and what's on your mind? Bible stories.

Hosea was the prophet whom God commanded to marry a prostitute. I once asked Father if God would ever tell someone today to do something like that. "No," he said. "That was a special revelation, so that Hosea could stand as a sign of God's faithfulness at a time when the people of Israel were whoring after foreign gods."

But if God commanded it once, why couldn't he do it again? His people weren't any more faithful today than they were in Bible times. Was God telling me to marry this girl?

I stared up at the ceiling and listened for God, but didn't hear anything—not even the girl's breathing.

The folks at Remus Baptist had a direct telephone line to God. "The Lord told me," they'd always say, or, "The Lord laid it on my heart." But God never spoke to me. I used to lie awake at night begging for a few words— even a simple "hello"—just so I'd know he was there, but I never got a peep out of him. Maybe it was just as well. If I ever heard the voice of God, I'd shit my britches.

According to my father, God's main way of speaking was through the Bible. And Hosea wasn't the only biblical precedent for marrying a loose woman. In Sunday school, they made it sound like the women of the Bible were a bunch of pious schoolmarms—but nothing could be further from the truth. Take Tamar, for instance. She disguises herself as a harlot and sleeps with her own father-in-law, just to prove what a hypocrite he is. Or Ruth. When Ruth spots a man she likes, she gets him drunk, strips off his clothes, and hops into bed with him. When he wakes up the next morning, he has no choice but to marry her.

And Tamar and Ruth weren't the fallen women of the Bible—they were the righteous ones. In fact, Matthew puts them on Jesus' family tree, along with that other seductress, Bathsheba. These women were Jesus' great-grandmothers! If they were alive today, I thought, you wouldn't find them at a Sunday school picnic. You'd be a lot more likely to find them in the Pink Palace.

If Father ever complained about me marrying a whore, I'd tell him to go read his Bible. What a day *that* would be.

I lay on the floor daydreaming about all this for quite a while. All this time, I didn't hear so much as a whisper from the bed above—the girl sure was a sound sleeper. Then I noticed that the door was slightly open. And next to the door, my extra change of clothes was strewn out on the floor. I climbed up to check the bed.

It was empty. I looked under the sheets, checked the other side, threw open the closet, searched every corner of the room. She was gone—and all my money with her.

I paced the room thinking about what to do next. I couldn't go downstairs and face the mademoiselle—she'd just laugh at me. There was a fire escape outside. I was terrified of heights, but that seemed like the best exit. I unlatched the window.

Then I heard a ruckus in the hallway—someone yelling and kicking and scratching at the walls. Another satisfied customer, I thought. The commotion grew louder and closer. I shook at the old window, trying to wrestle it open. But before I could escape, my door burst open. Mademoiselle Colette stomped into the room, dragging the girl behind.

The mademoiselle threw her onto the bed. "You little slut," she said. "We don't treat our customers this way." The girl's face was streaked with eye shadow and she had a new bruise on her arm.

Mademoiselle Colette handed me a wad of bills, then pressed her fat knee against the girl's chest. "Apologize to the gentleman," she demanded.

I grabbed the mademoiselle's hand and shoved the money back in her plump fingers. "She didn't steal it," I said. "Really—I gave it to her."

The mademoiselle released the girl and waddled backwards, leering at me. "She's not worth it."

I stepped between the two of them. "Well, I think she is." My voice was shaking. "It's my money, anyhow—isn't it for me to decide?"

"If that's what you want," Mademoiselle Colette laughed. "But I get my commission." She stuffed half of the money into her dress and threw the rest onto the floor. "Fuck her again," she growled. "Till you get your money's worth." Then she stomped out and slammed the door.

I picked up the bills and laid them on the bed, next to the girl. "Here you go," I said. "Keep it. Get out of here." She didn't say anything—just kept her face buried in the sheets. I wanted to ask if she'd come to Texas with me. I wanted to ask if she knew anything about raising chickens. But instead of asking another stupid question, I squeezed out the window and onto the fire escape.

CHAPTER 10

I DIDN'T HAVE SEX WITH THE GIRL, but I sure got screwed. There was no going to Texas without money. And there was no going back to Remus empty-handed, either. Even if the railroad let me return on credit, there was no way to pay it back—Father had given me the last of his money. And supposing I did go home, what would Father say? I could picture him shaking his bandaged head and saying, "As it is written in Proverbs, 'Many a man is brought low by a loose woman.'"

Why did I have to give that girl my money? I felt sorry for her, I wanted the hell out of there, and I was too flustered to stop and divide it between the two of us.

I bummed around town all morning, staring in shop windows and sitting on park benches. I went into restaurants and offered to wash dishes in exchange for food, like people in the movies always do, but no one would have me. In the afternoon, I swiped a bottle of warm milk off someone's porch. I took one swig and spit it out—it was as sour as an old sock.

Around dinnertime, the gray sky let loose with a cold drizzle. I sat under a tree and pulled my coat over my head, but it was no use. I was cold, broke, and lonesome. In other words, I had the blues.

I started humming a tune I'd once heard a logger sing back in Remus:

> *I got the blues so bad, the whole round world looks blue;*
> *I ain't got a dime, and I don't know what to do.*

Somehow, that made me feel a little better. It helped to know that I wasn't alone—lots of other guys had been down and out, just like me. And what did they do? They sure didn't sit around and mope.

> *When a woman gets the blues, she hangs her little head and cries;*
> *But when a man gets the blues, he grabs a train and rides.*

That's what Sammy Swisher did, and Eddie Quackenbush, and Bucky Hendershott—all my old friends. They'd
jumped freights and beat it out of town. I'd always been
too scared to try, but now there was no other choice.

By the time I got to the trainyards, the sky was pouring
buckets. I walked along the tracks, past rows of empty
boxcars, soaked through to the bone. Finally, I came to a
tin-roofed shed with an open door, and ducked inside for
shelter.

It was dark inside, so I was startled to get a welcome.
"Hey 'bo—got any grub?" When my eyes adjusted, I saw
five or six men huddled in a circle around a makeshift
stove. The air was thick with smoke and the smell of brew-
ing coffee.

I'd read a few stories about hoboes, so I was anxious
to try out their lingo. "Sorry," I said. "I'm busted. Flatter
than a pancake."

But instead of welcoming me as one of their own,
they looked away and muttered amongst themselves. "Awfully fancy duds for a 'bo," said one.

"Too soft for a bull," said another.

"Must be a punk," said a third. He turned and called
out to me—"Hey kid, where's yer jocker?"

They all laughed. I didn't know it at the time, but a jocker is an old hobo who lords over a young boy—or punk—forcing him to beg for handouts and do things you couldn't pay me to describe.

As I tried to explain myself, a Negro in a black overcoat walked over from the other side of the car and put his hand on my shoulder. "Don't waste your breath on these buzzards. They ain't worth a fart in a whirlwind."

He was tall and broad-shouldered, with a face creased and oily like worn leather. Between his white whiskers and lively eyes, he looked both ancient and ageless—a look I've only seen in black men. Atop his head was a frayed derby, just like Chaplin's.

"Name's Craw," he said. "What's your moniker?"

"Tobias. Tobias Henry."

He shook his head. "That'll never do, greenhorn. If you want to be a hobo, first thing you need is a proper moniker. Where you from?"

"Oh, you wouldn't know the place," I said.

"Try me, kid—I've been everywhere."

"Remus."

Craw looked up and scratched the whiskers under his chin.

"It's in Michigan," I said, trying to help him out.

"Damned if you've haven't stumped me," he said.

"Now—where was I . . . ?"

"You were saying I needed a moniker."

"Ah, yes." He put his left hand on my shoulder. "I hereby christen you . . . *the Remus Kid*."

I wished he hadn't. It was embarrassing enough to be from Remus. Even worse to be *called* Remus.

"How about Glen Rose, Texas," I asked. "Ever been there?"

"Sure have. In fact, I'm headed that way now—to Oklahoma, maybe on to Fort Worth."

My eyes widened. I didn't even know which train I needed to hop. But if I could follow this veteran . . .

"Mind if I tag along?" I asked.

"I'd enjoy the company."

When I held out my hand to shake, Craw pulled his right arm out of his pocket and held up a steel hook. "Lost it twenty years ago in Cincy," he said. "Last time I ever tried to shake hands with a brakeman." I shuddered at the thought—and the sight. "I assure you I'm quite harmless," he said. "Unless prodded, provoked, or otherwise perturbed."

We milled around for a while, till a whistle moaned in the distance. Everyone quieted down and straightened up. It was the Southern, Craw said, and that meant we were getting on board. "The metal will be slick—for God's sake and your mama's, step lively."

As I followed Craw towards the door, one of the hoboes laughed. "Looks like the punk found himself a jocker."

"Better watch out for ol' Craw," another told me. "He'll bugger anything with two legs."

Craw flashed his hook. "Shut your grub hole, or this'll be up your arse." The 'bo stopped laughing and backed off. "I'll have you know," Craw continued, "I've met some very fine one-legged women in my day. I even bagged a three-legger once, out in Frisco." He paused. "Ah, the things she could do with that leg."

Great—I was about to climb into a boxcar with an old pervert. Craw turned and gave me a wink—whether to assuage my fears or confirm them, I wasn't sure.

The whistle blew again, much louder. "So when you jump," I asked, "what exactly do you grab hold of?"

"A ladder," Craw said. "if you can find one. Just stick behind me and do just as I do. That is, unless I fall. If that happens, do the opposite."

As the train approached, it rattled the shed like an earthquake. The hoboes waited inside till the engine rolled by, so as not to be seen by the engineer. Then they spilled

out the door and scampered like a pack of gray rats to-
ward the train.

One man turned around and pushed his way back
inside. "It's rainin' like Billy-be-damned out there. I ain't
gonna break *my* neck." I looked to see if Craw had heard,
but he was already lumbering towards the train. I threw
my pack over my shoulder and followed.

The ground shook below and rain pounded down
from above. Boxcars and tankers whirred by with increas-
ing speed. Smoke and steam billowed out in thick clouds
that clung to the damp air. I could barely see Craw and
had to run my fastest to keep pace.

We ran alongside of a boxcar till Craw got even with
the ladder. Then he leapt up and hooked it. Hand over
hook, he climbed up the bars to make room for me. I came
as close to the spinning wheels as I could bear, then lunged
for the ladder with all I had.

Unfortunately, I didn't have much. I snagged a low
rung and my legs flew out from under me, whipping my
body to the side and slamming my gut against the edge of
the car. With all the wind knocked out of me, I hung there
limp as a ragdoll, my toes kicking against the gravel and
raindrops pelting my face like nails.

I reached for the next rung with my right hand. My
fingers slipped off the cold, wet bar and my arm fell to

the side, sending my pack tumbling under the train. I hung by only one hand now, and my arm felt like it was tearing out of its socket. I pictured that lone arm riding all the way to Texas, still holding on long after my body had been ground into hamburger.

On the bright side, no one would call me the Remus Kid ever again.

CHAPTER 11

THE NEXT THING I REMEMBER, my whole body was laid out flat and shaking on a boxcar floor. I couldn't see Craw's face in the darkness, but his voice was unmistakable. "Congratulations, my boy—you made it aboard with all your parts intact. So far as I can tell, that is. Whether or not you'll be able to have children is an open question."

I scooted back against the side of the car and rubbed my hands together, trying to bring some feeling back. "How did I get here?"

"Well," Craw said, "I was going to compose a ballad in memorium of your demise, but I couldn't decide whether it should be called 'The Remus Kid's Last Ride' or 'The Remus Kid's First Ride'—so I gave up and rescued you instead."

What I didn't understand was how he could have dragged me all the way up the ladder and into the car, especially with only one good hand.

Craw slid over next to me. "Hungry?"

"You bet—I haven't had a bite all day." My stomach growled to second the motion.

"Be grateful you had one yesterday," Craw said. "That's better than some folks." He pulled a silver tin out of his coat and peeled back the lid. With his hook, he speared a strip of pale, flaccid meat and dangled it in front of my face. The scent of lye burned my nose.

My stomach stopped growling and tightened into a knot. "What *is* it?"

"A Hoover steak." Craw slurped it down and fished me another piece.

I nibbled on the edge—it tasted like a piece of bologna that had met a violent death and been embalmed. "I take it you didn't vote for Hoover."

Sleeping in a boxcar was enough to make me miss my berth. When I woke up the next morning, I had to piss through a crack between the planks and hope that Craw's tastes were limited to women. But I wasn't in a position to complain about the accommodations.

Thankfully, the cracks in the walls were wide enough to let in some sun and provide a glimpse of the countryside, too. Missouri in May: it was the most beautiful land I'd ever seen—lush and green, with dew-drenched hills. We rolled on over mountains (maybe they were just hills, but they felt like mountains to me) and through cut-rock gorges. Craw called out all the stations from memory—Rolla, Lebanon, Joplin, Springfield.

After a while, he slid over next to me. "If I were your father," he said, "I'd be worried about you. Of course, I speak only hypothetically. I have no children—to my knowledge, at least."

"I didn't run away," I said. "My father's the one who sent me out. He got in an accident and lost his sight."

"I'm sorry," Craw said. "How did it happen?"

"A bird shat in his eyes."

He leaned in closer. "I can hardly hear with these old ears of mine. It sounded like you said—"

"Bird. Shat. He got drunk and passed out on the lawn. A bird flew over and—"

"Say no more," Craw said, putting his hand on my shoulder. "I know what it's like to have a drunk for a father."

"He's not a drunk," I said. "It was the only time he's ever touched the stuff. He's a Baptist preacher."

"*Say no more.*"

Craw scooted away and started carving at the wall with his hook. After a while, I saw he was carving a rhyme:

Baptists and Catholics, all have their creeds;
Still the doubt is, where true Christianity be.

"You're a poet?" I asked.

"No, but I dabble."

A minute later, Craw made his way to the back of the car to pee. He unzipped his pants and looked back over his shoulder. "My pecker's a poet."

"How's that?"

"He's a longfellow."

By now, I knew Craw was more a braggart than a pervert. When I asked him about his travels, he spun tales of riding the rails and stowing away on ships, bumming all the way from Alaska to Timbuktu and back—twice.

I asked if he'd ever been to France. "Oh yes," he said. "Those French women love black men."

"Why'd you ever leave?" If I could have gone to

live with the French Lady, I sure as heck wouldn't have come back.

"The ol' wanderlust, I suppose. Leaving's in my blood."

I wanted to hear more. "Is it true that all the ladies in France, you know, don't shave under their arms?"

Craw rubbed his chin. "I can't say for certain. You see, I didn't have time to inspect them all . . ."

"But as a general rule?"

"My boy, no woman in the world shaved her armpits till Mack Sennett's bathing beauties started the craze. That was back about nineteen-and-sixteen."

"1916?"

"That's right. I was nineteen, and the bathing beauties were sixteen. But that's a whole nuther story."

As the afternoon wore on, he asked more questions about my journey. "So what beckons you to Glen Rose?"

I hesitated. Lying is an important skill to have on the road, and I've always been terrible at it. My lips may say one thing, but my face always gives me away. And I surely didn't want any hobo to know about the money.

When I stammered, Craw nudged me with his elbow. "A girl, eh?"

"Heck no," I said. "It's only my uncle. He owns a farm, and my father's sending me to work for the summer."

"Be grateful you have a job waiting for you. That's better than most."

That gave me an idea. I needed a guide, and Craw needed money—maybe we could strike a deal. "If you're looking for work," I said, "I'll bet my uncle could use a extra hand."

Craw held up his hook. "So could I."

"Are you interested in work?"

"Work?" Craw snorted. "I've never worked a day in my life. Work is for chumps." He waved his hand around the boxcar. "Look at me—I've got everything a man could ask for."

My heart sank. There was no way I could make it to Glen Rose on my own. Even if I did make it there, I wasn't sure I could find the money. My father's map was shredded in a hundred pieces somewhere along the tracks in St. Louis.

For a long while, neither of us said anything. Then Craw picked at his empty tin can with his hook and tossed it across the car. "I've been thinking about your offer," he said. "Do you suppose your uncle could use the services of a carpenter?"

My eyes lit up. "I'm sure he would. So you're a carpenter?"

"No—but for a bed and two meals a day, I'm willing to learn."

Later that afternoon, we crossed over into Oklahoma. My throat was parched and my stomach so empty it didn't even bother growling anymore. My bones ached from the constant vibration, and my ass had long since gone numb. So when Craw said he was ready to get off for a break, I heartily agreed. "Next stop is Muskogee," he said. "There'll be friends there. And food."

He opened the hitch on the side door. "Let's hope your exit is better than your entrance," he said.

"You mean, we have to jump while the car's still moving at full speed?"

"We can't exactly ease into the station, waltz out, and wave hello like a couple of Hoover tourists. They'd throw us in the can."

Craw could tell I was worried. "Just follow my lead," he said. "Aim for the grass, watch out for the bushes, and don't forget to roll."

He slid open the door, tucked his hat under his arm,

yelled something—a prayer or a curse, I couldn't tell which—and shoved off. His body touched down with a thump and tumbled over the grass like a sack of laundry.

It sure looked easy. I took a deep breath, pinched my eyes shut, and jumped for all I was worth.

Which, once again, wasn't much. I hit the gravel face-first, flailed, bounced, and landed smack in the middle of a thistle bush.

It took a minute for Craw to catch up with me. "I said aim for the *grass*," he said. "Not land on your ass."

Warm blood ran out of my nose and lip and trickled down my chin. But instead of helping me up, Craw started rutting around in the weeds. "What are you doing?" I asked. "I'm bleeding to death, and you're picking wild-flowers?"

"To send back home to your mama," he said. "For your funeral."

I climbed to my feet like a groggy prizefighter. My clothes were torn at the knees and elbows, and my arms and legs burned with gravel scrapes and nettle stings. I swaggered around like I'd just survived nine rounds with Jack Dempsey.

Craw crumbled up a handful of weeds and squeezed

them till the juice came out. Then he took a chaw of tobacco, spit it over the weeds, and rubbed the mixture together in his hand. "Here," he said. "Put this on your wounds."

"Like heck," I said. "You're trying to kill me."

"It's ragweed and snuff," he said. "The best medicine there is to stop itching and bleeding."

I wasn't in the mood for some half-baked hillbilly cure. "Why don't you fetch some poison ivy while you're at it."

"Oh ye of little faith. Just *try* it. Unless you'd rather wait for an itinerant doctor to come riding up."

Eventually, I decided to humor him. After all, it couldn't sting any worse than the pricklers already did. I was wrong: when Craw smeared his concoction on my arm, it burned like the devil's poker.

"Give it a minute," Craw said. "You ever heard of a medicine that feels good at first?"

While I waited, he lectured me on the scientific method. "Everyone scoffs at a pioneer. Did you ever stop to consider the person who first discovered milk? It took a lot of nerve to be the first man to pull on a cow's nipple and drink whatever came out. You can bet his friends never let him live that down. And yet, a million years later, nobody thinks anything of drinking cow juice."

As it sank in, the ragweed-snuff salve went from fire to ice. To my astonishment, it was actually cool and soothing. Within five minutes, I could hardly feel my scrapes and scratches.

Craw was still talking. "If the world was full of skeptics like you, nobody would ever discover anything. Eggs, for instance. Would you have been first in line to eat a white ball that fell out of a hen's ass? I think not. But I bet you'd trade anything for a hardboiled egg right now."

When I asked for more salve, Craw beamed in triumph. Then he took some cigarette papers out of his pocket and told me to use them for bandages.

"My boy," Craw said, "I've been collecting cures since before you were born. I know all the secrets of Indian shamans, Voodoo witch doctors, and mountain grannies. For instance, a turpentine and lard poultice will clear up a chest cold. Blackberry juice and red oak bark stop diarrhea. If you've got the opposite problem, mayapple root will get your bowels moving. For worms in the stomach, eat crackled egg shells in syrup. Walnut hulls ward off ringworm. Milkweed for warts. Why, I can cure everything from baldness to flatulence."

I looked over at Craw's head—he was still carrying his hat. "But you're nearly bald."

He snapped his derby back on his head. "I said that I *know* the cures, not that I have all the necessary ingredients at hand."

Then he bent over, flipped up his coattails, and ripped a great fart.

CHAPTER 12

WE WALKED ALONG THE TRACKS for what seemed like miles, and I began to doubt whether Craw had any idea where we were. Now and then he'd stop and sniff the air. "We're almost there. I can almost smell it."

As far as I could see, there was nothing but red dirt and thistle bushes ahead. The sun was resting low on distant hills, casting a golden glow across the Oklahoma prairie. Back in Remus, it was probably raining icicles; who was I to complain?

After a while, Craw picked up the scent and turned off on a rabbit trail, through the knee-high grass and towards a row of scrubby trees.

"Smell that, boy?"

"What—did you mark your territory last time you were here?"

"*Smoke*, boy!"

I followed him through the trees and down into a gorge, towards a stream of water red as tomato juice. The air was pungent with the smell of dead fish, rotting vegetation—and smoke. Craw's nose was right.

Then I spied an encampment of sorts, up ahead under a cement bridge. There were four or five shanties pieced together from wooden pallets, sheets of tin, and boxcar doors. On the river bank, two hoboes flanked a cookstove made from a barrel with a grate on top. A plump hobo stood stirring, while his skinny companion sat hunched over on a milk crate.

Craw gave a sweeping bow. "Welcome to Hooverville." It looked more like a train wreck than a town, but all that mattered was the kettle of soup boiling on top of that stove. "We'll eat like kings tonight," Craw said. Then he called out— "Hey ho, jungle buzzards!"

The man stirring the soup dropped his ladle and hurried towards us. "Why, look what just washed up—you filthy old bastard, Craw!"

"When did you get out of the bughouse, Chester?"

After they exchanged a few more insults, Craw introduced me. "This here's the Remus Kid. As tough a greenhorn as ever rode the rails. Watch your language, though—he's a preacher's boy. I don't want to catch you taking the Lord's name in vain or saying damn or hell, neither."

"Damn it all to hell, Craw—them's half the words I know! Can't I say shit?"

"Of course you can say shit," Craw said. "That's not a curse—it's a colloquialism."

I tried to explain that Craw was only fooling and I didn't give a damn what the hell anyone said. "Aw, don't you mind us," Chester said. "I done got religion myself once. Just can't remember where I put it. And Craw, here—why, he knows the Good Book better'n any minister. He can recite all Ten Commandments by heart. Course, that's cause he's done broke 'em so many times."

"You've got to sin before you can be redeemed," Craw said. "A man might as well enjoy it."

All this while, the skinny hobo stayed put with his back to us. When we got closer, I saw he was hunched over grinding coffee beans between two stones. "That's Red," Chester said. "He's a comedian."

Red mumbled something. The words were indecipherable, but they sent Chester into a laughing fit. "Like I keep sayin', Red—they're gonna put you in the movies."

Red craned his neck around and grunted something vaguely threatening. When I saw his face, I stepped back; one of Red's eye sockets was an empty, shriveled hole. But Chester only laughed harder. "Cut it out with them jokes, dammit. I done warned you—you're gonna make me split my gut."

When we reached the stove, Craw leaned over the kettle and grinned. "This, my boy, is mulligan stew. Also known as sonuvabitch stew, when we're in impolite society."

The bubbling mixture was gray as ditchwater, swimming with unidentified chunks of white and brown. It wasn't Campbell's, but by this point I didn't care. "I'm so hungry I could eat a skunk," I said.

"Careful," Craw said. "You might just get your wish. Chester—what's in this gruel?"

"Oh, the usual," Chester said. "Potatoes, onions, beans, carrots, catfish, possum. And a snapping turtle—couldn't pry the shell off the devil, so I threw him in whole."

Craw took another sniff. "Dare I ask how long that possum has been deceased?"

"Red killed him fresh just this morning," Chester said, ladling the soup into tin cups. That was one detail I could have done without.

I took a sip. It tasted pretty good, actually, as long as I closed my eyes and pinched my nose.

"Fill up," Craw told me. "This might be our last grub for a while. Food on the road is as scarce as preachers in heaven—if you'll pardon the expression."

A few more hoboes straggled into the Muskogee jungle before nightfall, but none made an impression on me like Chester and Red. Chester looked like an overgrown baby, jolly and plump, with a head as bald as a billiards ball. Red was long and gaunt with sunken cheeks, an Adam's apple the size of a baseball, and a wild shock of orange hair. Chester did all the talking for the both of them, aside from Red's grunts. They were the Laurel and Hardy of hoboes.

When the ladle scraped the bottom of the kettle and our bellies were full, we gathered twigs and branches for a bonfire. Our ragtag company gathered around, about eight in all, and Craw regaled us with his songs. One of his ballads described a hobo's vision of heaven:

> *Where the cigarettes grow near whiskey streams,*
> *An' hamburgers sprout on trees;*
> *Where the chickens lay eggs right in your hand,*

An' lay down to roast in a fryin pan;
Where the cows churn butter in their pails,
An' pour you milk when you pull their tails;
Where pretty girls swim in the fountains,
In the Big Potato Mountains . . .

Another of his songs told the story of a hobo Don Juan whose exploits could have filled a dozen dirty comics. The ending went something like this:

Now Hobo Bill sits on his porch,
An' his wives play with his hair;
He sees the freight trains passin' by,
But he says 'Go on, I don't care.'

He's settled down, the old-time rambler,
An' he's got more wives than a priest;
He's loaded up higher than a riverboat gambler,
The dirty old bum of a beast.

As Craw sang, the other 'bos would interject an occasional shout or "amen." It wasn't much different from a Baptist camp meeting—except that instead of God and the Bible, he was singing about whiskey and women.

Red sat on a log next to me, but he kept silent. Amidst the revelry, he just sipped his coffee and stared at the dirt between his feet. I couldn't help but glance at his hands and imagine them tearing the skin off a live possum. But then he jerked up his head and caught me looking, with the one eyeball he had left. And once he latched that yellow, bloodshot orb on me, he wouldn't let go.

For the first time, he spoke. "I reckon Craw warned you about the ghost cow." The mention of a ghost wasn't as unnerving as Red's voice itself, which seemed to rise out of his chest and scrape against the sides of his throat on the way out.

"No," I said.

Red pointed a bony finger towards a tree at the edge of camp. "See that there skull?" There was a cracked, sun-bleached cow skull hanging on the trunk of the tree. I nodded.

"They used to drive cattle over this land," Red said. "One night a cow got separated from the herd and wandered into the river. The bed of this here river's like quicksand, and that cow sunk down till the water was up to her neck. Coyotes came and took her in the middle of the night. Picked her bones clean and carried off everything but the skull."

I pulled away from Red's eye long enough to look around the bonfire. All the other hoboes were in rapt attention to the story. Craw was gone—he must have stepped out to relieve himself.

Red went on. "Now, some nights you can hear a clanging bell, or a cow moaning from the middle of the river. I even seen it once—a cow's body, all pale and glowing, walking around with no head. That's why I hung the skull on that tree—so when she comes looking for her head, she can find it easy."

I glanced over at that white skull and a shiver went down my spine. Red had me scared out of my wits, and I didn't even believe in ghosts. This world is all there is, I tried to remind myself. Since there's no afterlife, nobody—human or cow—can return to haunt the living.

Then Craw returned, laughing. "Aw, not that ghost cow bullshit."

The veins in Red's neck swelled up. "You shut up, Craw. I seen him with my own eye."

"What were you drinking?"

Red spat in the fire and it sizzled. "You don't believe in spooks?"

"Course I believe in spooks," Craw said. "If, by that, you mean the shades of departed souls. But I don't believe in headless heifers."

As the fire died out, we settled into our separate shanties. Craw showed me how to make a bed out of newspapers—

Hoover blankets, he called them. Before he left me alone, I asked whether he'd ever seen a ghost.

"Certainly. In fact, I'm looking at one now." I looked back over my shoulder. "Why, *you're* a ghost," he said, "and so am I. We're spirits haunting these bodies of flesh and blood, just as spooks haunt houses of wood and stone."

"You believe in haunted houses?"

"All houses," he said, "wherein men have lived and died, are haunted houses.

> *Through open doors, the phantoms on their errands glide,*
> *With feet that make no sound upon the floors.*
>
> *We have no title-deeds to house or lands;*
> *Owners and occupants of earlier dates*
> *From graves forgotten stretch their dusty hands,*
> *And hold in mortmain still their old estates.*
>
> *The spirit-world around this world of sense*
> *Floats like an atmosphere, and everywhere*
> *Wafts through these earthly mists and vapors dense*
> *A vital breath of more ethereal air.*

One of the perks of being an atheist—or so I thought—was that I didn't have to be afraid of ghosts anymore. Growing up, I was so scared of ghosts that I could hardly sleep some nights. I'd tremble every time a branch scraped across my window, and shake at every creak of the hallway floor—just waiting for a spook to burst in. This was because Mama used to tell me her family's ghost stories.

Mama even claimed to have seen a spook with her own eyes. "When I was a little girl, I had a baby brother who drowned in the river. Papa made a gravemarker for him, but somehow it got broken in two. Papa didn't want to throw it out, so he put that broken gravestone under my bed. One night, I woke up to someone tickling my toes. There was a fat little boy—white as a sheet—standing at the foot of my bed, smiling. He didn't say anything at all, just smiled. I know it was my little brother, come back to tell me he was happy in heaven."

But Father always cut off Mama's stories. "There's no such thing as ghosts," he'd say. "When you die, you either go to heaven or hell. Nobody returns to this earth.

"But," Father was quick to add, "there *is* such a thing as demons. The Bible says they're fallen angels. When people think they've seen a ghost, it's really a demon sent by Satan to torment them." That didn't help comfort my night terrors.

Demons, ghosts, ghost cows—it's all pure superstition, I thought, lying there in the Muskogee jungle. Every supposedly supernatural phenomenon has a perfectly reasonable, natural explanation. To an inebriated, one-eyed hobo, a white dog becomes a ghost cow. The moonlight was probably playing tricks with Mama's eyes. As for Craw—this was a man who believed that eating eggshells would kill a tapeworm.

With all this thinking about spooks, I didn't sleep well. In the middle of the night, something startled me awake. It sounded like an animal outside my shanty. I lay there in terror, listening to the snorts and snarls. For what seemed like an hour, the sounds kept coming from the same spot, just a few feet from my flimsy shelter. Maybe Red was right about the ghost cow.

When it became apparent that the beast—whatever it was—wasn't going anywhere, I mustered enough courage to poke my head outside. There was no animal, living or deceased, to be seen. Instead, the noises seemed to be coming from Craw's shanty.

I crept over to the opening. There was no one but Craw inside, and he was face down and snoring. I shook his shoulder till he rolled over. "Do you hear those noises?"

"Sorry about the commotion," Craw said, rolling back onto his belly. "That's why they call it sonuvabitch stew."

CHAPTER 13

THE REMUS KID'S SECOND RIDE got off to a much better start than his first. As the sun rose, we hid at the top of a hill where the train would slow down. When the 'bos made their run, I kept close behind Craw. He leapt up, hooked the ladder, and held out his hand.

We climbed up top and dropped through the open hatch of the same boxcar as Red and Chester. It was an empty cattle car, the floor covered with hay and manure. Avoiding the shit as best we could, we piled the hay into beds. Craw leaned back and grinned. "Now this is what I call first class—cushioned seats!"

An hour or two into the ride, Chester lit up a half-burnt cigar and pulled an amber bottle out of his coat pocket. "I've been saving this for a special occasion," he said.

Craw jumped up. "Hot damn! What's the occasion?"

"There ain't one," Chester said, pulling out the cork. "But I got a terrible thirst and can't wait no longer." He took a swig and passed it to Craw.

Craw took one drink and grimaced. "This isn't whiskey—it's horse pee." Then he took another. "Damn fine horse, though."

"Tennessee bred," Chester said.

Craw lifted the bottle as if to make a toast. "The Tennessee stud—that's what the girls used to call me."

Red grabbed it out of Craw's hand and grunted. "Used to." (I was getting to where I could understand him now.) That got Chester laughing, till he choked on his cigar. "Damn it, Red—yer gonna be the death of me."

Red shoved the bottle between his lips and threw back his head. As he swallowed, his Adam's apple ran up and down his throat like a mouse. The bottle was halfway empty and draining fast.

Chester stopped laughing. "Gimme that, you red-haired bastard!" He tried to wrestle it out of Red's grip.

"Red hair's better'n no hair at all," Red growled. Whiskey splashed down his coat, but he wouldn't let go.

"I'll tear yer *other* eye out!" Chester yelled. He swung his fist and knocked the bottle out of Red's mouth—along with a bloody tooth. Red lunged forward and the two of them locked together, tumbling and cursing across the floor.

In the middle of the ruckus, Chester's burning cigar fell onto the whiskey-drenched hay. Craw stamped his feet at the flames, but they spread too fast. When they reached the bottle, it exploded in a shower of red-hot glass.

"Hellfire and tarnation!" Chester yelled, beating at his flaming sleeve. Soon, the whole back of the boxcar was on fire. Red—and I had no idea why—was struggling to unbuckle his pants. I stayed behind Craw, who rattled the sidedoor latch. "Locked, dammit!" He started hacking away at the wood with his hook.

The next thing I knew, Red had his pants around his ankles, standing there naked as Noah. Then he aimed his pecker at the flames and let loose with a shower. Chester cheered him on and urged me to join in. "Pee, boys, pee!"

It was no use. The flames only climbed higher. Red had so much alcohol in him that his piss was probably like kerosene. The entire car was hot as a tinderbox and filling up with smoke.

Finally, Craw knocked off the latch and the door swung open. I yelled for Craw to jump first. "Not this time. I've got to save their sorry asses," he said, pointing at Chester and Red. "As soon as they get their pants back on."

He shoved me forward. "Remember—aim for the grass!"

When you're flying in midair, having just jumped from a boxcar rolling at full speed, it's very difficult to aim for anything. Or maybe that's just my excuse. At any rate, I hit the gravel, bounced, and landed upside down in the dirt. At least I managed to dodge the bushes this time; my technique was improving.

I watched the rest of the train scream past, then climbed to my feet and waited for Craw. The cars rolled on, leaving a cloud of smoke hanging in the sky, and then the train was out of sight. *Why didn't he jump?*

I ran along the tracks till I was out of breath. About a mile down the line, I found Craw's derby; there was a hole burnt in the top. I tucked it under my arm and kept walking.

As the Oklahoma sun beat down, I felt as small and insignificant as an ant crawling in the middle of the

Sahara Desert. My throat was as dry and parched as the red dirt. Dust stung my cheeks and eyes.

The scene played over and over in my head: Chester and Red peeing. Craw fighting back the flames to drag them out. The three of them, trapped. The charred bodies. Red's burnt pecker.

I didn't cry—I never did, not even the day of Father's accident—but I felt like crying. It wasn't just that I was lost in the middle of nowhere, though that was bad enough.

I'd only known Craw for two days, but he was like a father to me. He was opposite my real father in every way—a black man who chewed snuff and drank whiskey and told dirty jokes—but he was like a father nonetheless. I missed the dirty old bum of a beast.

CHAPTER 14

IF I COULD HAVE TURNED BACK, I would have. I'd lost my money, Father's map—and now my guide. I had nothing left to lose but my life.

A couple hours later, another train whistled in the distance. I crouched behind a bush and waited. Part of me wanted to jump onto it; part of me wanted to jump in front of it. It probably wouldn't have made any difference. I let it steam past and kept walking.

Late afternoon, I came to a bridge over a river. Unlike the creek at the Muskogee jungle, this was a real river, at least a quarter mile across. I didn't dare cross a trestle that long on tired legs—no telling when another train would come along.

So I followed a trail down to the bank, cupped the warm water in my hands, and splashed the sweat and dust from my face. The sights and smells refreshed me. It was an oasis of life in a dry land—mayflies floating on the air, frogs splashing into the water, sunfish nipping bugs off the surface.

If only I had my fishing pole, I thought, I'd catch dinner in no time. As it was, the menu was limited. Mayflies make scant eating. Frog legs sounded appetizing—provided I could catch and cook the devils. For the next hour, I chased frogs along the bank, but all I managed to catch was a lumpy, bloated gray toad. Even after a full day without food, I wasn't *that* hungry.

When the sun started to set, I collected sticks for a fire. I'd never started a fire without matches, but I'd read about how to do it in boy's adventure magazines—all you do is rub the sticks together and puff on them.

After half an hour of lying on my belly, rubbing and puffing, I hadn't generated enough heat to melt a snowflake. If only I'd been a boy scout, I would have learned how to survive in the wild. Remus didn't have any boy scout troop. I suppose they didn't need one—your average Remus boy could kill and skin a buck with his bare hands. The problem was, I wasn't your average Remus boy—I was the pale, pansy preacher's son. All I could do in a pinch was recite a bunch of Goddamn Bible verses.

Finally, I jumped up, stomped around, yelled every curse word I knew, and hurled the sticks into the river. That made me feel a little better.

For the heck of it, I stuck a branch into the mud and hung Craw's hat on it. Then I started asking it questions. *What now, Craw? Try to hop another train? Find a house and beg? Swim out to a barge and hope they throw me a lifeline? Or just sit here and jerk off a few times before I die?*

Funny—I hadn't even thought about whacking the weasel for a week. That was a phenomenon even more amazing than Father being blinded by bird shit.

I wondered what jerking off would be called in hobo lingo. After a minute, I thought of the answer: "It's a Hoover fuck," I told Craw's hat. "A poor substitute for the real thing, but when it's all you've got it'll have to do. What do you say to that?" Craw thought that was pretty good.

I'd really gone over the edge now—talking to an empty hat about slapping the snake. What was worse, the hat started talking back. I heard it say my name—faintly at first, then louder. "Tobias . . ."

Hats don't talk, I told myself. Unless they happen to be haunted hats. That notion was more far fetched than a ghost cow.

But there it was again. "Tobias!"

Then I heard a rustling in the weeds. I spun around. "Craw?"

"Thank God," he said, "there you are!" As I reached out to shake his hand, Craw brushed right past me and took his derby from the stick. "I've been looking all over for you," he said, brushing it off. "I'm only half a man without my hat."

He screwed it onto his head and grinned. "Well, what are you staring at? You look like you've seen a ghost."

"Maybe I have." I wouldn't have been any more surprised if Jesus had appeared to me.

Craw raised his arms and twirled around. "I'm solid as ever, I assure you. Go ahead—touch me."

"But the fire—" I said. "How did you make it out?"

"Luckily, my coat's made of asbestos."

Then I remembered our comrades. "Where's Red and Chester?"

"They're hoofing it back to Muskogee, slightly fricasseed but none the worse for it. I had a hunch I'd find you at the river, and sure enough—I could hear you yelling from a mile away. I knew it was you, 'cause you cuss like a Baptist."

"Is that bad?"

"Well, it ain't good. It's like a Yankee trying to talk

Texan—you got the words right, but not the accent."

My face turned red. I couldn't catch my own supper, couldn't start a fire from sticks—now I couldn't even curse right. I was a complete failure as a hobo.

Craw patted my shoulder. "You'll get it someday. Just keep hanging around with riffraff like me."

It was dark now, except for the moonlight reflecting on the river. Craw showed me how to properly start a fire— it turned out that you have to find dry wood instead of pulling green twigs off trees.

"Now, if you'll excuse me," Craw said, "I've got to go lighten my load." He went off into the bushes and grunted—though I tried not to hear. Ten minutes later, he returned. "Take my advice," he said. "Don't get old. When I was your age, all I thought about was girls. When I was forty, all I thought about was money. These days, all I ask for is a good shit once a week."

I didn't ask whether he got his wish.

Craw slapped his leg. "Now—how about some food?"

My stomach rumbled at the word, but I didn't want to get my hopes up. "More Hoover steaks?"

"No," he said. "Catfish."

"And where are you going to get a catfish?"

Craw laughed. "We're sitting by a river chock full of them, aren't we?"

"True. But we don't have a pole, or line, or a hook, unless you're hiding something."

Craw held up his hook. "One out of three ain't bad. We don't need a pole, anyhow. Haven't you ever gone noodlin'?"

"*Noodling?* As in spaghetti?"

"As in barehanded fishing," Craw said. "At night, catfish burrow in holes to rest. Just wade into the river and feel your way along the bank, checking for holes. When you find one, reach inside. If you find a catfish, just grab it by the gills and grapple it up to the surface. Easy as pie."

I preferred to do my fishing from dry land. But Craw seemed hell-bent on this noodling, and I was hungry enough to try.

I took off my shoes and socks and rolled up my pants' legs. Craw laughed. "You're going to have to go in deeper than that."

Hoping this wasn't some perverse ploy to get me naked, I hid behind a tree and stripped down to my undershorts, then dropped into the water. Craw stood up above with his arms crossed, smirking.

"Well, are you coming in?" I asked.

"I'm spotting you," he said. "Someone's got to haul the fish up once you catch it." As unfair as it was, that suited me fine—I sure as hell didn't want to see Craw in *his* skivvies.

The warm water lapped against my skin, all the way up to my chest, and the river bed squished between my toes below. It didn't take long to find a hole, and it was close enough to the surface that I could reach inside without ducking my head underwater. I crouched down and stretched my arms forward, keeping my head just above water. Sure enough, the hole was inhabited. What luck— I could almost taste broiled catfish.

"I've got one!" I yelled up to Craw. As I tried to get a grip, it twisted and thrashed against my hands and fore- arms. Wherever I grabbed, I couldn't feel any gills.

"One thing I forgot to tell you," Craw said. "Watch out for snakes."

I didn't have time to listen—just then, my dinner shot out of its hole to make an escape. As it passed over my shoulder, I saw it wasn't a catfish at all. It was a water snake as big around as my arm.

I screamed and splashed, batting it away. "Damn! Shit! Hell!"

"It's all right," Craw said. "You scared him off."

Despite the warm water, I was cold and trembling. Besides ghosts, snakes had always been my biggest fear— and being an atheist didn't help that one. "Why didn't you warn me *before* I got in the water?"

"Look on the bright side," Craw said. "That snake did wonders for your cursing. You sounded like a natural that time."

That was scant consolation.

"Furthermore," Craw said, "it's a sure bet that you flushed out the only snake in the area."

"You *sure* of that?"

"Certainly—a water moccasin that size doesn't take kindly to neighbors." My arms were trembling, but Craw didn't show much concern. "Even if you *had* gotten bit," he said, "it wouldn't have been the end of the world. I know a surefire cure for snakebite."

"I'll bet you do." I made my way up river, eager to get away from that snake's den in case he decided to return home.

"Turpentine and milkweed poultice," Craw said. "Works every time, even on the most poisonous bites. Of course, I don't have any turpentine on me at the moment..."

After a little while, I found another hole. The opening was at least two feet in diameter—too large for a snake's home, I hoped. I reached inside, deeper and deeper. The water lapped against my neck, and then my chin, and then my lips—and still I hadn't reached the back of the hole.

Craw babbled on. "But there's always jackrabbit dung. That's easy to come by out in the wild. I once met a Cherokee Indian medicine man who swore by jackrabbit droppings for snakebite."

My fingers pressed against soft, slick flesh. I jumped back, and felt whiskers brush against my forearm. This was definitely not a snake.

"And if you think that's something, you wouldn't believe the things he could do with buffalo chips . . ."

My heart pounding, I eased my hand along the gills, wrapped my fingers around the sharp, bony edge, and tugged. At first, it didn't budge—I might as well have been trying to lift a boulder. Then it tugged back. It yanked my arms like a freight train, dragging my head underwater. I braced my legs against the sides of the hole and pulled with all my might. Which, as usual, wasn't much—but it was enough to get the fish riled.

When it came barreling out of its den, I wrapped my legs around its belly and rode that catfish like a bucking bronco. I gasped for breath as my head splashed in and out of water. Craw yelled from up above. "Holy sardines!"

The fish pinned my back against the riverbottom. I tried to pinch its thick, pulsing body between my legs, but water stung my nose and clogged my throat.

Then Craw jumped into the water and speared the fish through the nose with his hook.

As Craw dragged the flopping fish to land, I crawled behind coughing up water and sand. I collapsed on the bank, feeling like Jonah after he'd been spit up by the whale.

Craw beamed over our prize. "By damn, boy! You've caught the mother of all catfish!"

"I didn't catch her," I said. "She caught me."

Emerging from the river victorious, I was a new man. That channel cat was half as tall as me, and twice as big around in the belly. Craw carved enough meat off its body to feed an army—or at least two exceptionally hungry hoboes. Those succulent fillets, roasted over the campfire, were the best I've ever eaten.

After the feast, with bellies full, we basked in the fire's warmth. "You're a real hobo now," Craw said. "I've never seen anybody wrestle a monster like that and live to tell the tale."

"Maybe you'll write a ballad about it someday."

"A capital suggestion," Craw said. "The Remus Kid Meets the Okie Cat."

Craw didn't sing any ballads that night. But as he tended the fire, he elaborated on his philosophy of life.

"In every age," he said, "in every time and place, there are those who live on the margins of civilization. Outcasts, wanderers, searchers, hoboes—call them what you will. They stand outside of society, living by their own code. Knights of the road."

He threw some fresh twigs on the fire. "Out on the road, you meet all types of people—young and old, black and white, rich and poor, pious and depraved. And you begin to see that—at the core—we're all alike."

"How's that?"

"Ever seen a play?"

I shook my head. "My father wouldn't allow it. He says the theater is the devil's playhouse. Besides, Remus doesn't have one."

"Then you've never seen a movie?"

"Oh yes," I said. "I've snuck out and seen plenty of those."

"Well, imagine a movie—a vast production with kings, fools, knights, ladies, peasants, preachers, prostitutes—every sort of person you find in the world. When the actors take off their costumes, they're all equal. So it is with life. When death strips us of our roles, we're all equals in the grave."

"So where do hoboes fit in?"

Craw poked at the fire, sending up a shower of sparks. "It's easy for actors get to caught up their roles. So much so, they often forget that they're actors at all. Kings start believing that they have a divine right to rule. The rich lord over the poor as if its their right. But hoboes stay on the fringes, refusing to put on any costumes. We reject the gold and silk and finery of this life, preferring to stand as signs of contradiction—witnesses to the truth."

That made me think of my father. He'd always enjoyed playing the role of preacher, looking down on everybody else from his pulpit. But then his costume got torn off, and now he didn't know who he was anymore.

Craw leaned towards me, flames flickering against his face. "Remember this, my boy. The two greatest men who ever lived—Jesus and Socrates—were both hoboes."

It was strange to hear Craw mention Jesus. I didn't know much about the other fellow, but I remembered one thing from school—"They killed Socrates, too, didn't they?"

"That's right, my boy. Society always tries to enslave, imprison, and execute its greatest men, those who dare to stand apart and rise above." He scratched his chin.

"That's why I'm keeping a low profile—so the bastards don't get me."

Before we stretched out on the ground to sleep, I picked up the catfish carcass on a long branch and carried it towards the river. Gutted, it still weighed at least twenty pounds.

"Hold it!" Craw said. "I'm not done with that."

"But we picked it clean," I said. "There's not a morsel of meat left."

"It ain't meat I'm after."

When I dropped the carcass, Craw knelt down and picked through the innards with his hook. Then I realized what he must be doing. I moaned. "Don't tell me . . ."

"Scoff if you will, but there are more cures in a catfish liver than in a whole hospital. It's nature's best kept secret."

"It won't be a secret once the coyotes catch a whiff. Leaving fresh fish guts around the campsite—you might as well send them an invitation."

"Tobias, my boy—haven't you learned?" Craw spread a handkerchief on the ground, set the organs on it, and tied the corners together. "This world is full of wonders," he said, hoisting his treasure. "You just need the eyes to see them."

"And a nose to smell them," I said. "Do you realize how bad that's going to reek tomorrow?"

Craw reached up and tied the top of his handkerchief to a tree branch. "That'll keep it out of reach of animals. And don't you worry about the smell—it'll be dry by sunup."

CHAPTER 15

THE NEXT MORNING we crossed the trestle over the river—luckily, without meeting a train along the way. When we reached the other side, Craw broke out in song:

The stars at night
Are big and bright

"That's your cue," he said. "Start clapping."

I looked at him crossways. "It isn't night. And there's not a star in the sky."

"Don't you know where we are, boy? This here's the Red River. That means we're—

Clap-clap-clap!
Deep in the heart of Texas

"Well, not exactly deep in the heart," he added. "But we're over the threshold."

Texas. Craw might as well have told me that we'd just entered the Land of Oz. It was a mythical place for me—the land of cactuses and cowboys, the land of my ancestors. I couldn't believe I was really there.

We had to hitchhike the rest of the way. After the boxcar fire, Craw explained, bulls would be searching every train between Oklahoma and Fort Worth.

"Bulls?"

"Railroad cops."

"They're mean?"

Craw nodded. "And the meanest of them all is Texas Slim. He's killed at least twenty hoboes, some only boys. He'd pinch his own mother if she hopped a train."

And so we started along the highway, holding out our thumbs and choking on the dust kicked up by every passing car. After a couple of miles, I started wondering whether anyone would ever stop for two ragged hoboes. The pavement was baking hot and the air reeked of dead animals. Funny thing was, I couldn't see any dead animals—I just smelled them.

Then I realized what it was. "I *told* you it would smell."

"What?"

"Those catfish guts."

"I don't smell anything."

"That's because you never bathe. Your nose has lost the *ability* to smell."

Another car roared past.

"Nobody's going to pick us up with that stench," I said.

Craw stepped into the middle of the road. "Have some faith, boy." In the distance, a truck came into view. The closer it got, the faster it came—still, Craw didn't budge. Finally, about twenty feet away from turning Craw into roadkill, the driver slammed on the brakes. The tires screeched and swerved. As he passed us, the driver leaned out the window shaking his fist and cursing.

Craw tipped his hat, then turned to me and shrugged. "If I'd have known he was a doctor, I wouldn't have tried to stop him. He must be rushing to an emergency."

"Doctor? What are you talking about?"

"Sure—didn't you see the side of the truck? Doctor Pepper, Waco, Texas."

I shook my head. "All I saw was a soda pop bottle."

"Some day, my boy, Doctor Pepper might come to your rescue."

Eventually, the Texans took pity on us. We hitched our first ride in an empty livestock trailer headed to the Fort Worth stockyards—which gave us our second opportunity in as many days to ride on a bed of straw and shit. From there, a produce truck carried us to Granbury. Then, a Ford wagon brought us just outside Glen Rose, right up to the Henry family farm.

As the sun sank behind the hills, we walked up a long dirt drive, past some small houses, rows of apple trees (the apples were still green, but we couldn't resist picking a couple), animal pens, a rusty tractor, and a truck with "Henry Farms" on the door.

I looked over at Craw. "Remember—no one's supposed know about what happened to my father."

"My lips are sealed," Craw said.

Rounding a patch of scrubby trees, we found the farmhouse—a two-story limestone building with a wooden porch. The white stone was beautiful against the wide purple sky, and lights were burning in the downstairs windows. My heart leapt.

Up till that moment, I hadn't given any thought to how we looked. Two bums—one black, one white, and both so dirty you couldn't tell which was which—

drenched in sweat, clothes torn and burnt, reeking of cow shit and rotting fish, gnawing on stolen apples. How the hell was Wilburn supposed to know that I was his nephew?

Before we even reached the steps, a man in striped overalls kicked open the screen door and stepped onto the porch, rifle in hand. "No handouts here, fellas. You best be movin on."

A cigarette hung from the corner of his mouth. He was taller and stronger than my father, with a ruddy, weathered face. "I'm looking for Mr. Henry," I said.

Without saying a word, the man slowly raised the barrel of his gun.

"I'm his nephew," I said. "Tobias Henry. From Michigan."

Wilburn's jaw dropped open and his cigarette fell to the ground. "Well I'll be damned!" Then he lowered his gun, shook my hand, and slapped my shoulder. "Damn it all if you ain't Malachi's spittin image . . ."

He turned and eyed Craw. "Now don't tell me you're kin, too."

"Allow me to introduce myself," Craw said with a bow. "Cornelius McCraw, carpenter extraordinaire, at your service." It was the first time I ever heard his real name.

Uncle Will looked suspicious. "He's my guide," I said. "Without him, I'd have gotten killed—twice."

Craw kept his hook in his coat pocket. He held out his left hand to shake, but Wilburn ignored it and turned back to me. "What in tarnation are you doing in Texas?"

"Well," I said, "not much happens up in Remus, so Father sent me out to see his homeland and get some life experience."

Uncle Will gave a sharp laugh. "Last I knew, Malachi didn't have much use for life experience."

"He thinks I've had it easy," I said—and that was no lie. "He says it's time I learned to work the land and earn my own keep, the way he did growing up."

"The way *he* did?" Wilburn laughed again. "The only things Malachi ever worked at was singing songs and chasing skirts. Course, that was before he went off to preacher's school." Uncle Will leaned against the porch railing and lit up another cigarette.

A woman's voice called out from the house. "Wilburn? Wilburn—?"

"That's my Millie," he told me. Then he yelled back, "It's all right, darlin. Come on out here and meet the new hired hand—your nephew Tobias."

Millie pushed open the door, saw me, and gasped. "Why—Malachi's boy? Don't just stand there like an ass,

Wilburn—draw some water for a hot bath." She patted the front of my shirt, sending up a cloud of dust. "And fetch some fresh clothes out of Johnny's closet, while you're at it. I'll put some biscuits on—you boys must be famished."

"Boys?" Wilburn laughed, pointing at Craw. "That's the oldest boy I've ever seen."

Millie squinted her eyes, looked Craw up and down, and pulled Uncle Will inside the house. I could hear her through the screen door. "He's not setting foot in this house."

"But Millie—he's kin."

"Not Tobias. I'm talking about that nigger."

"Don't worry," Wilburn said. "I'll take care of it."

I hoped that Craw hadn't heard. If he did, he didn't say anything.

A few minutes later, Wilburn stepped out to explain the arrangements. "You can sleep in Jimmy's room," he told me. "He's our youngest. Room's been empty since he ran off to Fort Worth."

"What about Craw?" I asked.

Wilburn gazed out over his fields. "We don't have any other rooms," he said. I looked up at the house in disbelief—there must have been four bedrooms on the top floor. "But there's the barn," he said. "Or the shed."

"I thank you for your hospitality," Craw said. "But"
—I held my breath, expecting him to decline the offer
and take his leave—"I'd better take the shed. Otherwise,
I might disturb your cows with my snoring." *Whew*.

Just to be sure, I asked Uncle Will directly: "Does
this mean we have jobs for the summer?"

"I ain't as young as I used to be," he said. "Will Junior, my eldest, does most of the work now. I've got a hired
hand, but he ain't worth shootin. So—I suppose you can
take that as a yes."

"Craw, too?" I asked to be sure.

Wilburn glanced over. "He ain't as young as I used
to be, either."

"But I promised to help him. He saved my life."

"All right," Uncle Will said, giving up. "I reckon
he'll be good for something."

Later, Millie brought a batch of steaming biscuits out onto
the porch, along with butter and jam. Craw and I gobbled
them up—they tasted just like Mama's. At one point, Craw
uncovered his hook and speared two biscuits at once. Millie
jumped back at the sight.

When Millie left to get my room ready, Uncle Will
dragged a thin, yellow-stained mattress out of the cellar

and showed Craw to his shed. It was an unpainted clap-board structure with a sagging roof, not much bigger than an outhouse inside, and chock full of tools, machinery, and spare parts. Craw surveyed the premises. "It ain't exactly a Frank Lloyd Wright, but it'll do."

Back in the farmhouse, before I fell asleep, I heard Millie chastising Uncle Will. "I told you to get rid of him," she said. "And you give him a job?"

"But Millie—"

"He looks dangerous. For all we know, he could be a vicious criminal on the loose. Did you see that hook on his arm?"

"Aw, Millie—he's nothing but a harmless old coot. I know the type. As soon as he finds out how tough the work is, he'll be back on the road in no time. You can count on that."

I hoped he wasn't right. I didn't want to lose Craw again.

CHAPTER 16

AFTER A HEARTY BREAKFAST of ham and eggs, Uncle Will fitted me with some old leather boots. "Never go outside without these on," he said. "You've got to guard your ankles around here."

"From what—cactus?"

He laughed. "I reckon you don't have to worry much about rattlers in Michigan."

A chill crawled up my spine.

"But keep clear of the cacti, too. A jumpin' cactus can reach right out and bite you. And I don't care if you are kin—I ain't gonna be the one to pull the needles out of your ass."

After lunch, we all packed into the truck for a tour of the farm. I was stuck in the middle, crunched between Uncle Will's shoulders and Craw's. The main crop used to be cotton, Wilburn explained, before the topsoil dried up and blew away. Henry Farms survived by diversifying. We drove past row after row of fruit- and nut-bearing trees—apple, pear, peach, plum, orange, grapefruit, walnut, pecan. Among apples alone, Wilburn pointed out McIntosh, Cortland, King David, Jonathan, Smokehouse, and a dozen other varieties. Picking apples—now that sounded like a breezy way to spend the next month while searching for Father's money on the sly.

Uncle Will showed us the common garden, which was shared by him and Millie, Will Junior and his wife, and the hired hands. We went by the small houses Craw and I had seen last night—it turned out that Will Junior and the others lived in them. As we drove around, I kept an eye peeled for anything resembling an abandoned well. I thought about asking, but didn't want to arouse suspicion.

When we came to an open field, Wilburn shut off the truck. "This," he said, "is where you'll be spending most of your time."

What? It was a bare plain, all dirt and grass with not an apple tree in sight.

Wilburn turned to Craw. "You got any experience handling bulls?"

"Yes siree," Craw said. "I've been dodging them all my life."

I nudged Craw. "I think he means cows—not cops."

"The orchard's carried us through the depression," Wilburn said, "but fruits and nuts are chump change compared to cattle. That's where the real money is these days." He kicked back against his truck and lit up a cigarette. "Right this morning, Will Junior's checking out some bulls in Fort Worth. And I've got ten acres of pasture that needs to be fenced in before the first one arrives."

Putting up a fence would be more work than picking apples, but it still sounded easy enough. Of course, I had no idea how large an acre was. "Do you want us to do it right now?"

Wilburn spit out a cloud of smoke and slapped my back. "Atta boy! With an attitude like that, you'll go far. But truly, I'll be happy if you finish by the first of July."

Craw kept quiet for most of the tour—which was unusual for him. But he made up for it the next day when we started to work on the fence.

As I unrolled a bale of barbed wire, trying not to slice my fingers, Craw sat beneath the shade of a pecan tree, chopping rough branches into smooth fence posts. He steadied the branches with his hook and swung a hatchet with his hand. "This isn't exactly what I had in mind by *carpentry*."

I rolled up my sleeves and took a few whacks at the earth with a post-hole digger. The metal blade bounced off the hard ground, sending up a little cloud of dust.

After a while, I became aware of a constant buzz in the air. "What's that noise? Sounds like an electrical line."

"Cicadas," Craw said. "Also known as locusts. Or, as John the Baptist would say, *lunch*."

I laughed, surprised that Craw knew his Bible characters so well.

We hacked and hammered all morning. By noon, Craw had carved five fence posts and I had stuck two of them in the ground. I rested on the end of my digger and squinted up at the black birds circling overhead.

"Buzzards," Craw said.

After a few minutes, they swooped down to where I could see their gnarled, bald heads.

"They're waiting for us to die, aren't they? So they can pick our carcasses clean."

Craw tossed another finished post on his pile. "You

know, in all my years I've never encountered such pessimism in one so young."

"I don't trust birds," I said. "Not after what happened to my father."

"It's more than that," Craw said. "You don't seem to trust anyone. Here you are, entering the prime of life—a world of possibilities before you—and you're more cynical than Job."

First John the Baptist, now Job. "You read the Bible?" I asked.

"Not much. More often, I'd say it reads me."

"Take Job," I said, hoisting my post-hole digger. "He was the most faithful man on earth, and look what happened to him—his kids died, his flocks died, and his body got covered with boils. All because of a bet between God and the devil." I jammed my digger into the ground. "If I were around back then, I would have been one of the sons who got killed. And you blame me for being cynical?"

Craw chuckled. "No one ever said life was fair, did they?"

I threw down my post-hole digger and walked over to where he was sitting. I'd been waiting for an opportunity like this, to voice my doubts with someone who wouldn't judge me. I stammered around for a while, then dumped the whole load—the confused creation accounts,

Cain's wife, the flaming sword, the angels raping women, the dinosaurs getting left off the Ark.

By the end, I was shouting like my father on a Sunday morning. "Foreskins—*foreskins!* Can you believe it? How can *anyone* believe this stuff?"

I closed my case and waited for Craw to agree that it was all a farce, but he only smiled and shook his head. "You're going about it all wrong, my boy. You read Genesis like a textbook. It isn't science or history—it's a myth."

"You mean it's a lie," I said.

"Not at all."

"But a myth is a made-up story. A fairy tale. A *lie*."

Craw laughed. "That's the problem with you Baptists—

> *We both read the Bible day and night;*
> *But you read black where I read white!*

"Just because a story didn't actually *happen*," he continued, "you think it's a lie. But myths and fairy tales aren't lies—they're deeper truths."

"My father doesn't believe in stories," I said. "He says we should only believe in the facts. And to him, the Bible is a book of facts.

"Doesn't believe in *stories*? The Bible isn't a damn book of facts, it's a collection of stories. And Jesus wasn't a scientist or a mathematician—he was a storyteller." Craw threw up his hands. "Why, all of life is a story!"

"But if it's just a story," I said, "if all that stuff in Genesis didn't actually *happen*—how the hell can you say it's *true*?"

"Oftentimes," Craw said, "a truth is so big, so far beyond our understanding, that the only way we can grasp it is through a story. The creation of the whole universe is like that. How can our puny brains contain it?"

"So it's a lie . . . but it's a deeper truth. My brain can't even contain what you're saying."

"Hell," Craw said. "You don't believe Genesis is true-to-life? Show me a man and a woman in love, and I'll show you Adam and Eve. Give them a few weeks, and you'll have a fall from grace. A few years after that, Cain and Abel will be running around the house in diapers trying to kill each other. It's the plain stuff of life."

I began to see what he was getting at. But it still didn't explain a lot of things, like Abraham and the Jews. "What about circumcision?" I asked. "Where's the deeper truth in chopping the foreskin off your pecker?"

"It's a rite of passage, my boy. A mark of belonging

to the tribe." Craw picked up his hatchet and eyed the blade.

"Put that down," I said. "I've already been sliced."

He tossed it between my feet, laughing as I jumped back. "I hate to tell you this," he said, "but I doubt if it's even possible for you white folks to understand the Jews."

"Why not?"

"The Jews were tribal people. Nomads. Wanderers, fighting to keep their dignity. They were always being oppressed, exiled, sold into slavery. In America today, who does that remind you of?"

"Hoboes?"

"Not quite. I mean blacks. Negroes. Or—as your aunt would say—niggers."

My cheeks flushed red.

"The way I see it," Craw said, "white folks in this country have more in common with the Babylonians and Assyrians than the Jews."

I walked back to my digger, trying to avoid the subject. A minute later, I muttered under my breath. "I just need some proof, that's all."

Craw wiped the sweat from his brow. "Son, right now I could use a little proof myself. *Hundred* proof."

CHAPTER 17

EACH EVENING AFTER WORK, I'd wash my hands and go inside for dinner while Craw waited on the back porch for Millie to bring him a plate of food. I felt awful about it—especially after what Craw said about his people and the Jews—but Craw seemed grateful just to have regular meals.

And what meals they were! Fried chicken, pot roast, smoked ham, butternut squash, mashed potatoes slathered in butter, apple dumplings, hickorynut cake, squash pie. As soon as I licked my plate clean, she'd pile on another helping. She fussed over me like I was her own son. "Eat another piece of that pie before you waste away to nothing. What do they feed you up North—snow?"

While Uncle Will was laid-back, Millie was serious. Millie—no one dared call her Mildred—used to play the pump organ at the movie theater in downtown Glen Rose. She'd seen every Chaplin and Keaton film, but her favorite was Rudolph Valentino. In fact, she walked with a slight crick in her neck from years of looking over her shoulder at the screen while she played.

Once, I asked her which she liked better: silent movies or talkies. "Silent movies were an art," she said, "just like ballet. Talkies are just that—people talking. I wouldn't pay a nickel to hear anybody gab—not even Clark Gable. If I wanted to listen to a bunch of chattering, I'd go to the Bluebonnet Salon."

Millie was a woman of firm resolve and stubborn opinions. One evening, after she scolded Uncle Will for tracking dirt on the carpet, he snuck up behind her and pinched her ass. Millie jumped and screamed, "Wilburn Henry!" Then she looked at me, her face flustered pink. "He knows just how to get my goat."

Aunt Millie felt no need to be consistent in her judgments. For instance, she hated talking pictures but loved radio. Every evening, we gathered around the radio, which sat on a big table in the middle of the parlor. In my parents' house, that same spot was reserved for the family Bible. That summed up the difference between the two households—the radio stood for everything my father was against: worldly music, comedy, the Chesterfield Cigarettes program, and the brewery's "Old Foam Hour."

The farmhouse didn't have electricity, but Wilburn rigged up the radio to run on a car battery. We took turns choosing stations; Wilburn loved the Louisiana Hoedown and the Texas Roundup; Millie preferred Bing Crosby and Glen Miller; I wanted to hear Jack Benny and Burns & Allen.

"My father said you and him were in a music group," I told Uncle Will.

"That's right—the Golden Melody Makers. We still get together every once in a while, JP and me, my boys, and some of the cousins. In fact, you'll get to hear us in just a couple weeks—if you care to. The Henry family reunion's coming up in June, and we always put on a jamboree."

"You ever think of getting on the radio? I'll bet you could play on the Texas Roundup."

Wilburn laughed. "I'm too old for that. Besides, we ain't much to listen to without your father's voice. Damn, he was good. If only he hadn't gone all religious on us."

If only.

My first Sunday in Texas, I woke up and found an old suit of Jimmy's in the back of his closet. Jimmy was a strapping farm boy, and inside his suit I looked like a skeleton. When I came downstairs, Wilburn looked up over his coffee and smiled. "Where you going, boy? You look good enough to get buried."

"Don't you go to church?"

"Sure—for weddings and funerals."

"Oh Wilburn—don't you tease him." Millie handed me a steaming cup. "Tobias, you're welcome to borrow the car if you'd like to drive to church."

I considered the offer for a second—but only a second. "No thanks." After attending services three times a week for all of my life, I deserved a vacation. "I just assumed you'd be going, so—"

"We ain't churchgoing people," Wilburn said. "We're the sort of folks your father would call *lost*."

"I'm not my father," I said.

"I could see that from the start. If you acted like Malachi, I'd have already kicked your ass out of my house." At that, we both laughed.

"Last time I seen your father," Uncle Will said, "he was yelling at me to get on my knees and pray. It was some prayer he learned at Bible college—said if I didn't say this particular prayer, I'd go straight to hell. Well, I told Malachi that I'd rather go skinny dippin' in the Lake of Fire than to spend eternity with the likes of him."

I couldn't believe that anyone would say such a thing to my father's face—and I loved Wilburn for it. "What did he say to that?"

"Oh, he huffed that I was damned from the start and there was nothing he could do to help me. Some people are beyond the hope of grace, he said—that was another thing they taught him at Bible school. He went off to that seminary and came back acting all high and mighty, wanting us to call him 'Reverend Henry'—our own brother!"

"So the seminary changed him?"

"I'll say. They gave him a certificate, deputizing him to hunt down sinners and claim souls for Jesus. Well, there was nobody left to save around here, 'cept his own family—and we weren't falling for it. He had to go clear to the other end of the country before he found some folks who'd listen to him. We never heard much from him after that."

Uncle Will set down his coffee and looked out the window. "A few years back, when Pa passed on, I sent Malachi a letter. Told him Ma wanted him to come down and see her. But he never wrote back."

It still stung Wilburn, I could tell, and I felt sick that my father had done such a thing. *He deserved to be blinded.*

CHAPTER 18

AFTER A WEEK AT THE HENRY FARM, I was no closer to finding Father's money than when I'd first arrived. But I had gotten plenty of life experience; I'd learned how to lay a barbed-wire fence, how big ten acres is, and that it would take the rest of my life to enclose the latter with the former. My neck and ears were sunburnt to the point of peeling, and I woke up one morning with red sores on my ankles and crotch. They were *chiggers*— little bugs that hide in your socks and underwear and then burrow under your skin. Millie said that they can live off your flesh for months if you don't suffocate them; she gave me some ladies' nail polish to paint over the bites, which stung like the devil.

Another day, I sat on the john and felt something like a needle prick my bottom. I jumped up and there, crawling out from under the seat, was a scorpion the size of my pinky. All I knew about scorpions was that they were poisonous, and thought I was going to die—no one was going to suck the poison out of my ass, that much was sure. I ran into the farmhouse with my pants hanging down around my knees. "I'm stung! Poisoned!"

When Uncle Will surmised what had happened, he just laughed. "A little scorpion can't kill you."

At least Aunt Millie took some sympathy—she brought me some ice to put on the bite and a bromide fizz to drink. "The poison might upset your tummy," she said.

I was starting to see some good aspects of life in Remus: it was too cold for flesh-eating bugs or ass-biting insects.

That second week, I began searching in earnest for Father's money. Instead of going straight to dinner after work, I left Craw to explore the farm on my own. I cursed my luck for losing the map; with it, I'd have already found that well. I wanted to tell Craw about the money and enlist his help, but I couldn't. Who knew how much or how little money Father had buried? I couldn't promise anyone a cut.

On my second or third day of searching, I ventured to the far north end of the farm, which was bordered by a row of tall cedars. Sweaty and aching after a day of digging holes, the sound of rushing water lured me onward.

Beyond the trees and down a steep gorge was the Paluxy River. It was like nothing I'd ever seen—a swath of pure, blue water winding between huge slabs of chalky white limestone, set off against lush evergreens and bright green cacti. I slid down the hill and entered another world, far from Wilburn's dusty fields.

I wound my way between the big rocks and scampered over the smaller ones, till I reached the shore. Leaving my boots behind, I waded into the shallows. The water flowed around my ankles, warming my feet and cooling my body at the same time. In a spot where the stone formed a deep pocket, I spotted a school of bluegills—next time, I'd have to see if I could borrow a fishing pole from Uncle Will.

Then I got a strange urge—strange for me, at least. I peeled off all of my sweaty clothes and jumped into the water. When I was in up to my waist, I held out my arms and leaned back, gliding weightless on a sparkling bed of sapphire blue. All of my aches and pains melted away.

I wondered why I'd never liked swimming before.

Then I remembered that the waters in Northern Michigan are ice-cold even in summer, they're full of green slime and brown muck, and there's a good reason why the pond near our house was called Leach Lake.

After twenty minutes or so, I climbed back on shore and gathered up my clothes and boots. The sun was still shining through the trees on the other side, so I decided to climb onto a rock and bake till I was dry. I'd never seen rocks so big, and I felt like a mountain climber scaling them. I've always been afraid of heights, so when I reached the top I crouched down, afraid to stand and look over the edge. A ten-foot drop was more than enough to give me the shivers.

I stretched out on a slab of limestone, closed my eyes, and listened to the bubbling water and the buzz of cicadas. It was a strange feeling, being naked in the open air. For as long as I could remember, I'd been embarassed over my body and more than happy to keep it hidden. In fact, I'd only been naked out-of-doors once before—and that was in a desperate attempt to grow pubic hair. When I was fourteen, Eddie Quackenbush told me that cod liver oil was a magical hair-growth stimulant. "I put some on my sister when she was asleep," he claimed, "and a patch of hair sprouted up right before my eyes. When she woke up, boy was she steamed."

So I snuck out into the woods with a bottle of Squibb's Cod Liver Oil, laid naked on a pile of leaves, and slathered it on my chest, arms, and privates. Of course, nothing happened. But the next day, I told Eddie, "You're sure right about that oil. Now I've got more hair between my legs than the Wild Man of Borneo."

That got him back good—he went home and took a bath in the stuff.

Lying there above the Paluxy River, I looked down my chest at the scant patch of hair between my legs. At least I had *something* now. My chin was another story—I hadn't shaved for two weeks, and I was just now getting a five o-clock shadow.

From body hair, my thoughts turned to home. I wondered what my parents were doing right now and how Mama was taking it. She probably thought I was dead. In just over a month, they'd be kicked out of their home and shipped off to the poorhouse. To save them, I needed to find Father's money and bring it back—but after what Uncle Will had said, I was less sure than ever about returning home. My father didn't lift a finger to help his own mother in her hour of need—why should I help him? But there was Mama, too . . . if I didn't try to help her, how would I be any different from my father?

I dreamed of what I'd do with all that money, all to

myself. First thing, I'd buy a long, black Rolls Royce. And I'd get some fancy duds to match—a pinstriped suit and patent leather Oxfords. When Emily Apple saw me cruising down the street, she'd curse the day she met Lars Lundgren. She'd beg me to take her away, but I'd brush her off and say, "I loved you before you had breasts; you should have loved me before I got money." Then I'd leave her in a cloud of dust and go find the French Lady, whom I'd track down from the studio name on her postcard.

The dream was so vivid that, even when I was roused by the sound of an animal moving through the brush behind me, I swore it was the French Lady I saw scampering over another rock and making her way to the river. Maybe the sun was getting to me.

I squinted, blinked, and squeezed my eyes shut, but when I opened them again, she was still there—a real, flesh-and-blood girl in a black dress, walking along the shore. I flipped over onto my belly and scooted around to get a better look. Good thing I was laying flat, or she would have seen me already.

The girl dipped her toes into the water and watched the ripples she made. I couldn't see her face, but her hair was as black as her dress. She bent down to look at her reflection—or something under the water?—and then dropped to her knees. As the river lapped against her waist, she curled forward, pressing her face into her hands. Her shoulders started to shake—was she crying?

Next thing I knew, she was wailing and screaming and slashing at the water like a girl possessed. Finally, exhausted, she threw herself forward into the river. The water was only a foot deep, but that was enough to cover her almost entirely.

I wanted to call out, to ask if she was all right, but then I remembered that I was naked. More than that, my body was having its natural reaction to seeing a girl splashing in water. The flag pole was rising, completely oblivious to the possibility that she was in danger—and equally oblivious to the fact that I was lying flat on a slab of stone.

She floated face down in the water for what seemed like an eternity, the current tugging at her hair and dress. Then her head broke the surface, coughing and gasping, and she struggled up onto her hands and knees. When she rose to her feet, her whole body was shaking and her dress clung to her black and shiny as a seal's skin. She yelled something that I couldn't quite make out, but it sounded like, "Dammit—I *am* cursed!"

As she trudged back to shore, I scooted to the far end of my rock and laid low. I kept my cheek pressed against the rough stone—breathing heavy, heart pounding—while she scurried between the rocks, up the hill, and out of sight.

Even after she was gone, an electrical charge hung in the air. Every hair on my body was tingling, and all my senses were buzzing. Or was it just the cicadas?

CHAPTER 19

I DIDN'T TELL CRAW about what I'd seen at the river—unlike him, I wasn't one to talk about every woman I'd ever laid eyes on. But the image of that girl, floating in the water like a dark mermaid, stuck in my mind.

A couple days later, we were back at work in the field, whittling posts, digging holes, and stringing wire. It was the hottest one yet—not even June, and it must have been a hundred degrees. Sweat dripped off my hair and ran down my face, stinging my eyes, and my throat was as parched as the dirt under my feet.

About noon, when the sun was directly overhead,

Craw threw down his hatchet. "Holy leaping lizards . . ."

It sounded like he'd cut himself, but I didn't see any blood. "What's wrong?"

"The dementia's coming on," he said. "I always wondered which would go first—my mind or my body. Thank God it's my mind. At least I'll be comforted by visions of virgins in my final days."

"What the heck are you talking about?"

"You can't see her," he said. "She's only a figment of my fancy."

But when I turned around, there she was coming towards us—the mermaid girl, wearing the same black dress. "You aren't the only one hallucinating." Against her hip, she carried a clay jug wrapped in white cloth. It was filled to the brim, and as she stepped water sloshed out and dripped down the hem of her dress.

"It ain't real," Craw said. "It's one of those visions a dying man sees in a desert—a mirror—mira—oh, what the hell do you call it?"

Mirage or not, Craw rushed past me. "Old men first." He grabbed the jug, tipped it back, and gurgled till the water ran down his chin.

"Better slow down," the girl said, "or your friend will have to drink it off your shirt."

Finally, Craw passed me the half-empty jug and

wiped his mouth on his sleeve. "It ain't whiskey, but it ain't bad."

I was too nervous to look the girl in the face. As I took a sip, Craw removed his derby and gave a deep bow. "Are you an angel? Sent to comfort me in my dying hour?"

The girl laughed. "I'm no angel—I'm Sarah Hawthorn. Mister Henry sent me to keep you from dying of thirst."

I was too stunned to take it all in. A girl about my age, living right there on the farm—why hadn't Wilburn and Millie mentioned her before?

"I thank you mightily," Craw said. "It's hot enough to bake a horny toad. Of course, I can handle it fine—I have the endurance of a camel. But young Tobias here was on the verge of collapse."

She turned to me. "You're Mister Henry's nephew, right?" But before I could answer, Craw cut in. "You'll have to excuse my young friend. He's a bit, shall we say, girl shy."

Mortified, I stared down at the ground, hoping to find a hole into which to crawl and die. "Uncle Will—yes—that is, he's my uncle."

After an awkward silence, Sarah took the empty jug and turned to leave. "Well, I'd better get going. I've got to water the goats next."

Craw moaned like he'd been stabbed in the gut. "Now I see how it is. We're just two more animals that need watering. Is that all we are to you?"

She smiled and kept walking.

Craw called after her. "Why don't you fetch us some hay while you're at it? And a bucket of slop, too?"

"Just don't ask me to clean up after you," Sarah yelled back over her shoulder. "You'll have to shovel your own shit."

Craw whistled. "Now *there's* a girl."

Craw poked me with the round side of his hook. "Don't you feel it, boy?"

I was still wondering what she'd been doing at the river the day before. "Feel what?"

"What a girl can do—bring a ray of sunshine to the cloudiest day."

I squinted up at the sun. "Cloudiest day? You *are* hallucinating."

"It's a figure of speech, my boy. What I mean is— look at *that*." Craw pointed at Sarah in the distance, jug swinging against her hip.

I shook my head. "What are you staring at?"

"Nothing refreshes the spirit like a pretty girl with nice jugs."

"That's enough." I waved him off and started back to our fence.

"What? It was very nice of her to bring us a jug of water, that's all."

I bent down and picked up my post-hole digger. "You know—you could be that girl's father."

"If she takes after her mother, I surely could be."

I spun around, digger in hand. "You're a disgrace. Practically throwing yourself at a girl half your age. No—a quarter of your age, if that."

"Me? You actually thought that I—?" Craw gave me the same wounded look he'd given Sarah. "Believe me, son—I have no interest in her for myself. I was only trying to help *you.*"

I jammed my blade against the ground. "Well, for your future reference, I don't need any help. I can do a fine job of embarrassing myself."

"You certainly can," Craw spat. "A boy your age letting a pretty girl pass unnoticed—now *that's* disgraceful. You didn't even look at her face."

"Neither did you. You leered at all of her *but* her face."

Craw picked up his hatchet. "Tobias, my boy, a woman is the crown of creation. Remember—Adam was only God's rough draft, but Eve was his masterpiece. And if you don't appreciate God's masterpiece—why, that's what I call blasphemy."

Later that afternoon, Wilburn drove out to inspect our work. Cigarette hanging from his lip, he squinted at our ragtag assemblage of wire and posts. "The bad news is, that fence couldn't hold a blind bull with no legs. The worse news is, I've got three healthy bulls arriving in four weeks."

My jaw dropped to the ground. Craw lowered his head and clasped his derby over his heart. We'd been doing our best—could it really be that bad?

Uncle Will came up from behind and put his hand on our shoulders. "What's wrong? You two look like you're standing over a grave."

"We are," Craw said. "Mine."

Wilburn laughed. "Chin up! Moping never got nobody nowhere. Besides—ain't nothing a beer can't fix." He walked back to his truck door, rummaged around inside, and returned with three brown bottles.

Craw's face lit up and he snapped his derby back on his head. "Friends, Texans, countrymen—lend me a beer!" When Wilburn tossed him a bottle, he popped off the cap with his bare teeth.

Uncle Will started to hand me a bottle, then pulled back. "I suppose you won't want one of these, being a good Baptist and all."

Truth was, I'd never tasted beer. But at the challenge, I grabbed the bottle out of his hand, put the cap in my mouth, and chomped down. My two front teeth about cracked in half. Thankfully, Uncle Will had a bottle opener in his bib pocket, and he popped it for me.

I was thirsty as the devil, so I pressed the cold bottle to my lips and took a great swig. It smelled like moldy bread, but it went down fine. Then, somewhere between my throat and my stomach, it started foaming up. I felt it foaming higher and higher, till it exploded out of my nose in a shower of suds.

Uncle Will slapped my back. "Easy there, pardner!"

Craw held up his bottle to toast. "You know what our nation's great founding father, Benjamin Franklin, said? 'Beer is proof that God loves us and wants us to be happy.'"

"Amen to that," Wilburn said. "But if God made beer, why don't preachers drink it?"

"Good question." Craw rubbed his chin. "They ought to—it's a very spiritual beverage. One of the saints said that, in the middle of heaven, there's a great lake of beer where Jesus and the redeemed drink for all eternity."

Uncle Will leaned in closer. "Who said that?"

"Saint Brigid of Ireland."

Wilburn laughed. "Irish—that explains it."

My head felt tired and fuzzy, in a good way. For someone as skinny as me, I thought, it must take only a few drinks to get sloshed. I had to concentrate to make sure my words came out straight. "Why would God want us to be happy? According to my father, he wants us to be miserable."

Craw took another swig. "Imagine if you were God—a stretch, I know. But would you want your creatures to grovel around your feet all day, or enjoy all the gifts you've given them? Jesus himself drank wine—it's right there in the Bible. Hell, he couldn't stand the taste of water. When they brought him a barrel of the stuff, he turned it into wine. He spent so much time in taverns that the Pharisees called him a drunk."

"Damned if that don't beat all," Uncle Will said. "I never heard that in any church."

"The problem with a lot of church people," Craw said, "is that they're trying to be holier than Jesus."

Why did alcohol help Wilburn and Craw relax, but it drove my father crazy? Maybe it was because Father saw it as a temptation from the devil, instead of a gift from God. Anyhow, the beer was working wonders for Uncle Will and Craw—they'd never gotten along so well.

"Say, Cornelius," Wilburn said, "what did you say your family name was?"

"The great Scottish clan of McCraw."

"Funny—you don't look Scottish."

Craw slurped the last drop of foam from his bottle. "You've never seen me in my kilt."

Wilburn laughed and put his arm around Craw's shoulder. "Well, Brother McCraw, you ought to be a preacher. Cause the way you talk about Jesus, he sounds like somebody I'd like to have a drink with."

CHAPTER 20

THE NEXT SATURDAY was market day in Glen Rose, and Wilburn gave Craw and me a new assignment that not even we could mess up—or so he hoped. We loaded up the Ford wagon with eggs and butter, Millie's fresh-baked bread and pies, canned jams and fruit preserves, and several barrels of the season's first apples. At the last minute, though, Uncle Will thought twice about sending us alone. Maybe he didn't trust Craw with his money, or maybe he didn't trust me to keep all the prices straight, or maybe he didn't trust either of us to find our way to the courthouse square. Whatever his reasons, I was glad—

because a few minutes later, Sarah came walking up the dusty path.

Craw greeted her with a flurry of bows, prostrations, and kisses of the hand, while I held back, stealing glances out of the corner of my eye. I wasn't smitten by Sarah, but I was intrigued by her. This was the third time I'd seen her, and once again she was wearing that same tattered black dress. Had someone died, or was it just the only thing she owned?

Uncle Will had given me the key, but I was out of practice; Father never let me behind the wheel of his new Plymouth. To avoid making a fool of myself, I passed the key to Craw and the three of us crammed onto the hard seat, with Sarah in the middle. "Off we go," Craw said, jamming the key into the ignition and pumping the pedals. When nothing happened, he started throwing switches and pulling levers.

"Are you sure you've driven before?" Sarah asked.

"Course I have!" Craw jiggled the steering wheel with his hook. "I'm not used to these newfangled models, that's all."

Sarah crossed her arms and looked out my window. "This thing's at least ten years old. That may be new by your standards, but—"

Craw pounded his fist on the dashboard. "And I

suppose you could do better, little lady?"

"As a matter of fact—I could." With that, Sarah shoved against Craw and the door burst open; out he tumbled, sprawling in the dirt. She turned the key and pushed a pedal, and the engine then roared to life.

Craw walked around the truck and climbed in through the passenger door, cursing and muttering. "Girls these days, I swear . . ."

"Can't handle the newfangled ones, eh?" Sarah beamed triumphantly and stomped on the gas.

⚜

We peeled out of the drive and onto the dirt road, Wilburn's old truck rocking and teetering. There was no roof on the cab, so the wind and dust whipped against our faces. Every time we rounded a curve, I took a deep breath and hoped that Millie's pies wouldn't go airborne.

A couple miles down the road, Sarah slammed on the brakes and sent all the produce and baked goods— and me and Craw—jolting forward. Being the tallest, Craw's head slammed against the glass. "Shit! What the hell are you trying to do—kill me?"

"Quiet," Sarah said. "You'll startle him."

Craw rubbed his forehead. "*Him*—?"

When the dust cleared, we saw a strange creature

sitting in the middle of the road. It looked like a possum wearing a suit of armor. "What is it?" I asked.

"I'll be damned," Craw said. "A Hoover hog!"

Sarah hopped out, bent down, and picked up the beast. She brought it back to show me, cradling and stroking it like a baby. "You've never seen an armadillo before?"

"I've never even heard of such a thing." I turned to Craw—"You eat these?"

"Nah," Craw said. "I tried once, but it took all night to peel the shell off and there wasn't enough meat inside to—"

"That's disgusting!" Sarah spun around and carried her pet to the side of the road. "Don't you listen to that mean old man," she whispered, petting it on the head; then she set down the armadillo and sent it on his way. "There you go, little fella. Run along home."

As we watched it waddle through the grass, Craw couldn't resist. "Damn it all—there goes my lunch."

Sarah just glared at him.

It was an awful quiet ride into Glen Rose. Sarah's cheeks were red with anger, and Craw was afraid to get her riled when she was behind the wheel—he just braced himself against the dash and let out a sigh of relief at every stop sign.

When we got to the courthouse, Craw unloaded the heaviest crates and then left to explore the town. Wilburn had given us our two-weeks' wages that morning—a nickel for every day we'd worked—and Craw was anxious to spend his.

"It ain't often I get to buy instead of beg," he said. "I'm used to getting by on charm alone."

Sarah looked up from arranging pies. "You must go hungry a lot."

"There's something about me the ladies can't resist," Craw continued. "Pure animal magnetism, that's what I call it."

Sarah huffed. "*Animal* is right."

Craw straightened his derby, gave a bow, and turned to leave. "Don't you two try any funny business while I'm gone," he said. "I'm supposed to be chaperoning."

There was no chance of that, but my cheeks turned red at the suggestion. The truth was, I was glad to be left alone with Sarah—though not for any reason Craw could have guessed. She was a mystery that I wanted to solve.

For the next half hour, I carried baskets and boxes and set them down wherever Sarah pointed. When she wasn't watching, I studied her. Despite the way Craw acted around her, she wasn't the sort of girl you'd call pretty. She was small-framed, with gangly arms and legs and freckles all over. Her most striking feature was her crow black hair, but it was chopped short and left to fend for itself.

Business was brisk all morning, so we didn't have much time to talk. Which suited me fine—I've never been much of a talker. But I liked listening to Sarah, even when she was just naming off prices and chatting with customers about the weather. Most Southern girls' accents are too sickly sweet for me to stomach, but Sarah's voice had an edge of Texas toughness.

When the clock struck noon, Sarah suggested that we take a stroll around the square. On the courthouse lawn, old men sat at tables, reading newspapers and playing checkers. They spoke in a low rumble that broke into laughter at the end of every sentence, and then trailed off in a hacking cough. Old women sat on benches, sweating and fanning themselves. As we passed by, their conversation hushed to a whisper and they exchanged glances over the tops of their fans.

Outside the Bluebonnet Salon, one woman's fan in particular caught my eye. On the front, it said "Jesus Saves—Calvary Baptist Tabernacle." The back said "Garfield's Tea—Cures Constipation." I stood mesmerized as these two messages swished back and forth, till Sarah dragged me away by the sleeve.

Next, we came to the pawn shop. A sign in the window caught my eye:

WANTED:
Jewelry, Watches,
Guns, Gold Teeth.
Highest Prices Paid.

I peered inside and saw Craw haggling with the pawnbroker.

Sarah tugged my arm. "Quick—let's go before he sees us."

"Craw's really not so bad," I said. "He's just full of hot air sometimes, that's all." She didn't look convinced.

A few stores down, Sarah stopped in front of the apothecary. "Wait here." A minute later, she emerged with a tall, frosty glass. "A fresh-squeezed limeade—with a real maraschino cherry." She lifted out the cherry and dangled it in front of my face. "You'll have to fight me for it." Before I could say a word, she popped it between her teeth, snapped off the stem, and squeezed her lips shut. As she chewed, a trail of red juice dribbled out the corner of her mouth.

"You look like a vampire." I wiped it away with my

thumb. It was a terrible thing to say to a girl, but I didn't know what you're supposed to say when you touch a girl's face for the first time. My thumb still tingled.

She shot me one of her deadly stares. "You'd better watch out—maybe I am."

Cold and tangy on my tongue, that cherry limeade was the best thing I'd ever tasted. It went straight to my bloodstream and it chilled me all over. We passed the glass back and forth till there was nothing but ice left in the bottom, then we crunched the ice.

Back at the truck, we devoured some summer sausage and split a pie for lunch. In between bites, Sarah squinted at me and repeated my name. "Tobias . . . *Tobias* . . ."

"What?"

"Oh nothing," she said. "It's just that you have a funny name."

I wasn't sure whether to take that as an insult or a compliment. "Well, it's not as funny as Craw's real name—Cornelius."

"But it fits him. He deserves it. But you—you don't look like a Tobias. It sounds like an old man's name. Doesn't anyone ever call you Toby?"

I winced. "Not since I was a kid—and I hated it even then. At least Tobias sounds dignified."

Sarah took another bite of apple pie and smiled. "I like Toby. I think it's cute."

"*Cute*—that's exactly the problem. Puppies are cute. Kittens are cute. I don't want to be cute."

"Well, puppy or not—I'm going to call you Toby."

First the Remus Kid, now Toby the Puppy. This was not a good year for nicknames. I chewed my pie, racking my brain for a way to get her back. "You do that," I said, "and I'll call you Magpie."

Sarah frowned. "I hate my hair."

"Sorry—I was only fooling." I'd forgotten how touchy girls could be. "Really, I like black hair." It was the truth, but it didn't help.

"You can have it then," she said, flipping her fingers through her hair. "It gets hot as hell in the sun—I'd cut it *all* off if Mama would let me."

"Looks like you've made a good start."

It was about the tenth stupid thing I'd said that day— I began to remember why I usually kept my mouth shut around girls. Desperate to find a way out of the hole I was digging, I leaned forward and touched the top of her head. "I like short hair, too. I think it's cute."

Her frown broke into a smile. "Cute. Like Toby."

She had me now. Toby it was.

Despite her odd looks, something about Sarah captured my fancy. Maybe it was her eyes. On first glance, they looked buggy—too large and round for her face. On second glance, they seemed sad and deep. On third glance, they caught me looking—and I suddenly took an intense interest in a jar of strawberry preserves.

After lunch, Craw sauntered up to us wearing a grin as big as Texas. "Howdy, y'all! How do I look?" I hardly recognized him—his fire-tinged black derby was gone, and in its place was a huge, silvery-white cowboy hat. Even Sarah smiled at the transformation.

"I rode my ol hoss up to the trading post," he said. "Don't you laugh, boy—I said *hoss*. And I done brought back some fancy dry goods for y'all."

"I hope they didn't charge you for that accent," Sarah said. "You got gypped."

Craw asked me to close my eyes, then put a silver Lone Star belt buckle in my hands. "That there's to hold your chaps up."

Then he asked Sarah to do the same, and he slipped a beaded necklace over her head. When she opened her eyes, she laughed. "This isn't a necklace, silly. It's a rosary."

"Well, I thought it was mighty purdy," Craw said. "Just like you."

Sarah slid her fingers over the wooden beads and the gold crucifix. "It is pretty," she said. "The nuns gave me one when I was a girl, but I lost it years ago." Then she threw her arms around Craw's neck.

The lucky bastard—he *did* have a way with women.

"Well I'm glad you like it," he said. "Cause it cost me half my wages and three gold teeth."

At afternoon's end, we loaded the empty crates onto the truck and got ready to head home. Craw was on his best behavior—he didn't even argue when I gave Sarah the key. I sat in the middle again, pressed up against Sarah. Of course, I was pressed up against Craw, too, but my mind was on Sarah.

As the truck rumbled over the bumpy road, her sun-warmed hair brushed against my cheek. I closed my eyes and breathed in her scent; it was warm and fresh, like a cat that's been lounging in the sun. A girl would probably be insulted if you told her she smelled like a cat, but to me that's a compliment.

Just a couple miles from the farm, we hit what felt like a log in the middle of the road. Sarah let out a sharp yell and ground the brakes to a stop. "Dammit," she said, "I didn't see it coming."

"What the hell was that?" Craw asked. "Another Hoover hog?"

"If it was," I told Sarah, "you'd better not look back. It won't be a pretty sight."

Sarah closed her eyes and pressed her forehead against the wheel. "I hope I didn't bust a tire. Mister Henry will not be happy."

I volunteered to get out and check. The front tires looked fine, and when I walked to the back I didn't see any slaughtered armadillo in the road. I gave the rear tires a kick, then knelt down and peered under the truck bed. "I see something. Looks like a pipe fell off."

From up front, I heard Sarah groan. I got down on my belly and slid my head under the truck. Not only was there a large pipe on the ground, the truck was making a strange sound, too.

"Kill the engine," I yelled.

Sarah yelled back. "It's already off."

"Well you must've really busted it," I said, "cause the damn thing's still rattling." I crawled forward, dragging my belly over the dirt, and stretched my arm towards the pipe.

Finally, my fingers made contact. It felt too soft to be a pipe—a rubber hose? The rattling noise grew louder. And then it moved its head. It wasn't a pipe, or a hose—

it was a rattlesnake with a body as big around as my thigh.

I leapt off the ground and banged the back of my head against the truck bottom. As I scrambled backwards, the snake followed, his neck gliding towards me. I jumped to my feet and waved my arms, slowly stepping backwards.

Craw turned around in his seat. "What the devil's got into you, boy?"

Afraid to make a sound, I mouthed the word— "S-N-A-K-E."

Sarah looked at me sideways. "Cat got your tongue?"

The rattler poked its head out from under the truck. That diamond-shaped head was bigger than my fist. Desperate, I whispered—"*Sssnaaake*" and made a slithering motion with my hands.

Craw scratched his head. "Schnook? Schnape?"

But Sarah's eyes widened. "Don't move."

She ducked under the seat, then surfaced with a rifle. Craw threw up his hands. "Whatever this game is, I give up." Agile as a cat, Sarah jumped onto the back of the truck and hopped over the crates.

Below, the great snake coiled and lifted its head to strike. Above, Sarah steadied the gun on her shoulder. It seemed to be pointed directly between my legs. I saw her rosary glinting in the sun, Jesus swinging back and forth between her breasts—then I pinched my eyes shut and braced myself for God's judgment on my sex-obsessed mind. The only question was whether my manhood would be destroyed by snakebite or gunshot. One moment more, and I'd never have to think about that part of me again.

My eardrums burst and a shower of gravel peppered my face. A second shot exploded at my feet, then a third. I couldn't see anything for the dust. Sarah jumped off the truck, ran to edge of the road, and fired two more times into the grass. "Damn it all—he got away!"

My whole body was numb and trembling at the same time. I grabbed my crotch to make sure everything was still there. Yes, thank God, she'd missed.

CHAPTER 21

IF CRAW WAS RIGHT about old houses being haunted, the Henry farmhouse was especially so. It was built in the 1860s, and several generations of Henrys had left their footprints and fingerprints on the wooden floors and plaster walls. Walking down the hall to my room, I passed under the watchful eyes of my ancestors—rugged, stern men and women staring out from gilded frames. Many nights, I lay awake with the sense that I wasn't alone; but that didn't frighten me as long as I didn't see any dead people walking around.

The day after the market, though, I was jolted awake by the sound of a screaming baby. I sat up in bed shaking and sweating, waiting to hear it again, but the only sound was the creaking windmill. Must have been a dream, I thought—probably brought on by seeing that snake. I relaxed against the headboard and waited for my heart to calm down.

Then—*"Mama! MaaMaaa!"*

That, sure as hell, was not a dream. I jumped out of bed, threw on my pants, and ran down the stairs.

When I threw open the back door, there was Sarah wrestling in the dirt with a little white goat. She gave a startled gasp and the goat broke away. "Dammit—you spooked me!"

I rested on my knees, panting. "Your goat spooked *me*. It sounded like a baby screaming out here."

Sarah laughed. "They do sound like babies—I guess that's why they're called kids. But thanks to you, I've got to catch him again." She spun around, stamped her foot, and called out, "Hoppy! Hoppy, you come over here this instant!" Then she looked back at me. "Well, don't just stand there, Toby."

And so the two of us ran across the yard chasing the escaped goat. Finally, I cornered him against the cellar. "Give it up, Hoppy—you can't run forever." I crouched down. "We won't rest till you're back in the pen. You think you can make a break for Mexico? Our guards will gun you down."

Sarah ran up from behind. "Trying to reason with a goat?"

"Shhh," I said. "It's just a stall tactic. Get the lasso ready." As we kept perfectly still, Hoppy bent down to chomp a tuft of grass. "Now!"

Sarah tossed her rope and pulled it snug around his neck. The goat leapt and kicked but it was no use—we had him. In our moment of celebration, I hoped for a hug. "We make a good team." I glanced at her.

Sarah reached out and slapped my shoulder. "Sure do—you and Hoppy."

❧❧❧

I followed Sarah to the animal pens. "So you're here every morning? What all do you do?"

She yanked the wayward goat back in line. "Come along. I'll show you."

After Hoppy was safely behind bars, Sarah tossed some fresh hay to the goats. I grabbed some straw and fed a couple kids out of my hand. "Do you have names for all the animals?" I asked.

"No—just Hoppy. I call him that cause he's always hopping over the fence." She pitched another armful of hay over the fence. "Then there's Old Squeal, the hog. But I don't have to deal with him, thank God. Mister Henry feeds him all the scraps and leftovers."

Next, we walked to the chicken pen and Sarah gave me some corn to feed them. As soon as the kernels hit the ground, a large, redheaded chicken pushed all the others out of the way and snatched them up. "Wow—I'll bet you get some big eggs out of that one," I said.

Sarah laughed. "Don't you know the difference between a hen and a rooster?" My cheeks flushed—I didn't even know about sex in the animal world.

She pointed to a smaller, black chicken in the corner. "He's the only other male. All the rest are girls."

"What happened to his tail?"

"The big one pecked all his feathers off, just to show him who's boss." She sighed. "Boys—they're all alike."

Sarah ducked inside the hen house for a minute and collected a basketful of eggs. Then we headed back to the goat pen. "Milking time," she said.

"Don't ask me to help—I can't tell the girls from the boys."

Sarah led a mama goat with a heavy, swinging udder out of the pen and over to the milking bench. "Sure you don't want to try? It's easy—just watch." She grabbed two nipples and pulled them back and forth; soon, her pail was half-filled with frothing milk.

She stood up and pointed to the bench. "Your turn." When it became clear that she wasn't going to take no for an answer, I squatted down on the bench and gingerly wrapped my fingers around warm goat flesh. I couldn't help but wonder: if she kicked me in the head, would I see Jesus like my father had?

I didn't want to tell Sarah, but it was the first time I'd ever touched anyone's nipples. They were soft as suede leather and stretchy as rubber. Did girls' nipples feel like that, too?

I gave a tug, but nothing came out. "I think this one's empty."

"There's plenty left," Sarah said. "You've just got to pull harder."

So I tugged again. And again. Finally, the goat bleated—*"Maaaa!"*—reared back, and gave a mighty kick. The pail went flying and I tumbled over backwards.

I didn't see Jesus, but I did get a good soaking. Milk streamed down my shirt and pants, and I knew there was no way was I going to get a hug from Sarah now. When I turned to face her, she was bent over laughing. Her collar hung low enough that I could glimpse her breasts jiggling like two apples on a wind-tossed branch—and that lovely sight made all my humiliation worthwhile.

I got out of the way while Sarah finished the job. I couldn't blame the goat for not wanting me to pull her nipples—even an animal could tell that I didn't understand the first thing about breasts.

I was obsessed with breasts, but I had no idea why. I still am, and still don't. What are they, anyway? Built-in baby bottles. So why are they so attractive? Is it their roundness and softness? If women had only one breast and several nipples, like a goat, would breasts lose their charm? If women had udders on their bellies that swayed as they walked, would men still watch and whistle?

All I know is that a woman's breasts are the centerpiece of all that's beautiful, intriguing, and delightful about her. It's true even of small-chested girls like Sarah.

After Sarah filled two pails (or, rather, the goat filled them), we carried the milk and eggs back to the cooling shed. Wilburn and Millie didn't have an electric freezer, so they kept a small shed packed with ice blocks buried in straw to make them last. Sarah put one pail of milk and most of the eggs inside, but kept the rest out. "I have to take these back to Mama," she said.

It was a long walk down to the houses where the hired help live, but I volunteered to go along. Being Sunday, there wasn't any work that I needed to be doing; and besides, there wasn't anything else on the farm as interesting as Sarah.

As she gathered up the eggs in the front of her dress, I picked up the pail. "I'll carry the milk."

"All right," she said. "Just see that you don't spill it again."

"*I'm* not the one who kicked over the bucket—your goat did."

"But you provoked her."

It was no use trying to get the last word in.

As we started towards Sarah's house, the sun was low in the sky and the orchards shrouded in fog. This was about the time of morning I was usually just rolling out of bed; no wonder Craw and I hadn't run into her before.

"What sort of work does your father do on the farm?" I asked.

Sarah kept walking, staring straight ahead into the mist. I thought she hadn't heard. Then she looked down at the path. "My daddy died when I was ten."

"I'm sorry." We were both quiet for a while, but my mind was racing. Was that why Wilburn and Millie hadn't mentioned her family? Had she worn black every day since then?

"I don't remember much about Daddy," Sarah said, "Just the way he looked in the field that last summer, bent over hoeing cotton. And how tired he was."

"Was—was it an accident?"

Sarah shook her head. "One day, he just collapsed. His heart gave out on him."

I felt sick. "Did my uncle work him too hard?"

"No—Mister Henry was the only fair employer Daddy ever had. But by the time we got here, it was too late. After he was gone, Mister Henry let my mama and me stay on and do odd jobs. If it wasn't for him, I don't know where we'd be. "

I wished I could give her a hug. "Where did you live before here?"

Sarah gave a short laugh. "Where *didn't* we live? Daddy went wherever there was work, and Mama and I went with him. Georgia, Arizona, California. We lived in tents, boxcars, labor camps. Never had a home, really."

"I've lived in the same place my whole life—Remus, Michigan."

"You're lucky."

"Obviously you haven't been to Remus." I looked over at Sarah, but she didn't smile.

"There's nothing glamorous about life on the road," she said. "Daddy saw things that drained all the joy out of life."

"Like what?"

"Men killing each other over a watch or a key chain. Babies starving cause their mothers' milk went dry. He once saw a man selling his wife—a penny for ten minutes. He kept her in a boxcar, and men were lined up around the trainyard waiting their turn."

"That's awful." I thought about the things I'd seen in just a week on the road: the girl in St. Louis, Red's empty eye socket, the boxcar fire.

"Sometimes," Sarah said, "life on the farm isn't any easier. I've seen some things, too. That's the problem with life—no matter where you go, you can't escape death."

For the first time since we'd started walking, she looked at me. Her eyes seemed even larger than usual, and I saw my silhouette reflected on their watery sheen. Looking at those eyes was like glimpsing the surface of a dark pool—I had no idea how deep it ran, or what lurked inside. And I knew that if I fell in, I might never come back up.

"Watch it," she said. "You're spilling."

"Hold on." I set down the pail and brushed off my

pant leg. "It was only a drop. You just worry about your eggs."

Her fingers gripped the front of her dress, cradling the eggs inside. A single, clear drop fell onto her wrist and trickled down her hand. Then another tear melted into her dress. I reached out and put my trembling hand on her shoulder. Sarah fell against me and nestled her head under my chin. Her tears fell hot against my neck and soaked into my shirt. She sobbed until her whole body was shaking—the same way I'd seen her cry at the river— and I had no idea what to do about it. Was I supposed to cheer her up? Or try to help somehow?

The next thing I knew, my own eyes started watering. I wrapped my arms around Sarah's back, pressed my face into her hair, and tried to choke back the tears. But everything I'd been holding inside for the past month came bursting out.

Or, at least, half of me cried. The other half floated above, taking note of the sensations—blurry vision, burning nose, the taste of saltwater—and thinking, *So this is what it feels like. How strange—and girls do this all the time?*

Then I felt something wet against my crotch. *Dear God, did I wet my pants, too?*

Sarah pushed away, catching her breath between sniffles. "Oh, shit—the eggs."

We both stared down at the mess of clear goo, yellow yolk, and cracked shells oozing down the front of her dress. But I wasn't about to let that interrupt my hug. I pulled Sarah back into a salty, snotty, squashed-egg embrace, and kissed the top of her head.

CHAPTER 22

EVERY MORNING for the rest of the week, I woke up early to help Sarah with her chores—not that she needed the help. We didn't talk about what had happened on Sunday. We didn't talk about much of anything. But I felt a connection with her, and I thought she felt it, too. Maybe it was that neither of us had any brothers or sisters; it gets lonely being an only child.

I didn't breathe a word about her to anyone, but it didn't take long for Craw to get curious. I always met him at his shed with a plate of Millie's ham and eggs before heading out to work, but on Tuesday and Wednesday, I was a few minutes later than usual. Thursday, I missed him altogether. When I arrived at the work site an hour late, Craw was sitting on his usual stump hacking away at a post. He tipped his cowboy hat and grinned. "Must be something awful important keeping you these days."

I brushed past him, post-hole digger in hand. "Nope—just slept in."

"Now that's funny," Craw said. "Wilburn said you left the house at six."

I kept my back to him. "I had to feed the chickens, too."

"I'll bet it ain't just chickens you're spending time with."

"You're right," I said, jamming the digger into the ground. "It's the goats, too. You know—I've developed a new fondness for goats."

He chuckled. "Son, there's nothing to be ashamed of. You may be inexperienced, but you'll learn quick."

I kept quiet, frustrated that I couldn't keep a secret for one damn week. Besides—I liked being around Sarah, but that didn't mean that I was in love with her. She intrigued me, but she scared the hell out of me sometimes, too. You can never feel entirely at ease around a girl once you've seen her fire a rifle, especially if it was aimed between your legs.

"Ask me anything," Craw said. "There's nothing worth knowing about women that old Craw don't know."

I leaned on the digger handle. "All right—why do they cry so much?"

"Damned if I know."

"And what's a man supposed to do when a woman cries?"

"Go out and get a beer."

I shook my head and took another stab at the ground. "Maybe we should stick to making fences."

"Nah—too damn complicated."

Every time I talked to Sarah, I looked for a chance to slip in the question—"Do you know of any dry wells around here?"—but it never seemed to fit. I knew what would happen: she'd ask why I wanted to know, and it wouldn't take a minute for her to squeeze the whole truth out of me.

Time was short—my parents would be evicted in only three weeks. But as the days wore on, I thought less and less about the money. After work, instead of searching for the well during the two free hours before dinner, I started visiting Sarah's home on the far edge of the farm. It was a three-room, tin-roofed house painted bright canary yellow. "That was Mama's idea," Sarah said.

Sarah's mother, Rosalind Hawthorn, had long, deep red hair streaked with silver, which she kept braided and coiled on top of her head like a snake. The first time I met her, Rosalind was at the kitchen table rolling dough with an empty Doctor Pepper bottle. "Sarah's always had a special way with animals," she said. "She gets along better with critters than people. Land's sakes, the things she's brought home for pets—lizards, horned toads, snapping turtles, even scorpions. Once, when she was just a baby, I found her playing in the dirt with a black widow spider. She had it on a stick, hanging by a thread. She said, 'Look Mama, doesn't this spider have the prettiest red spot on her bottom?' I about died."

Sarah rolled her eyes. "But you didn't. And neither did I."

"Only because of the spirit watching over you," Rosalind said.

Sarah frowned. "That's enough, Mama."

Rosalind took the lid from a Mason jar and started cutting circles out of the dough. "I hope you can stay for biscuits, Toby."

As much as I hated being called Toby, I could *always* stay for biscuits. While they baked, I asked how it was that Sarah had black hair when Rosalind had red.

"I'm Irish," Rosalind said. "But John—Sarah's father—was part Spanish and a quarter Indian. His grandmother was a full-blooded Commanche princess. She was
the most amazing lady I've ever met, and she lived to be a
hundred and one. The day Sarah was born, she—"

Sarah grabbed her mother's arm. "Not that story,
Mama. *Please.*"

Rosalind got up to check the biscuits in the oven.
"Folks in Glen Rose gave us a hard time when we first
moved here," she said when she sat back down. "Some of
the old men fought the Commanches fifty years ago, and
they weren't ready to give up just yet. Thank God, most
of them have died off now."

The only decoration on the wall was a cardboard print
of a girl dressed all in black, holding a bundle of roses.
When Rosalind went outside to draw some water, I asked
Sarah who it was.

"That's Mama's favorite saint. Therese—the Little
Flower."

"She's young," I said.

"Yeah. She coughed up a bunch of blood and died
when she was twenty."

"How . . . saintly."

Saint Therese smiled out from her frame, but Sarah
gazed back with sad eyes. "Sometimes, I think it would

be nice to go that way," she said. "Maybe they'd paint pictures of me, too."

I glanced at the rosary beads around Sarah's neck. My father would have been horrified. According to him, Catholics were hell-bound idolaters. Even worse, they were cannibals. When they took communion, they actually believed they were gnawing on Jesus—every wafer was supposed to be a chunk of his thigh or forearm.

It didn't make any difference to me, but I asked just to be sure. "So you're Catholic?"

Sarah hesitated. "Yes. Maybe. I don't know."

I laughed. "You're not sure?"

"Mama goes to mass a couple times a year. I used to go with her, but not lately. We don't have a car, and the nearest parish—San Juan Baptist's—is half an hour's walk."

San Juan Baptist. Why did that sound familiar? "Wait a minute," I said. "Does that mean John the Baptist?"

"Sure—Saint John the Baptist."

I started laughing.

"What's so funny?"

"John the Baptist wasn't Catholic. He was the very first Baptist—everybody knows that."

Sarah shook her head. "They called him 'the Baptist' because he *baptized* people, silly."

I tapped my fingers on the table. "He swore off women, refused decent food and clothing, and was always yelling at people to repent. If that isn't Baptist, I don't know what is."

"He lived in the desert because he was a monk," Sarah said, putting her hand on top of mine. "Baptists don't even have monks."

The moment she touched me, I lost my train of thought. All I could do was smile and say, "Maybe you're right."

Baptist Catholics in Texas—who knew? Maybe my father would have approved after all.

CHAPTER 23

THAT SUNDAY, June 7th, was the Henry Family Reunion. Uncle Will described it as the highlight of the whole year—"There'll be music, square dancing, a hog roast, and buckets of beer"—and he and Millie spent the whole week getting ready. This was my chance to meet a slew of relatives I hadn't seen since I was a baby—including my grandmother.

Granny left the farm after Grandpa died; now she lived in Dallas with Aunt Ellabelle. "Ma likes to be close to the action," Uncle Will said. "She loves the shows, the taverns, the salons. She's practically bald, but Lord knows, every hair she's got left gets dyed and curled every week."

The day before the reunion, Old Squeal the hog met his demise. Saturday morning, Craw and I carried buckets of water to fill a huge cast-iron pot, and Millie lit a fire underneath. Once the water was boiling, Wilburn led Old Squeal to the oak tree, lassoed him to a sturdy branch, shot him twice, and hoisted up his body. Then he cut the hog's belly from top to bottom, spilling all the entrails onto the ground. I was glad Sarah wasn't there—as much as she disliked Old Squeal, she wouldn't have wanted to see what was left after his spirit flew up to hog heaven.

I glanced at Craw. "You going to salvage any of that? You know, for medicinal purposes?"

He looked as pale as a black man can get. "Don't make me lose my lunch."

"Why's it any different from catfish guts?"

"A fish is a clean animal. It doesn't wallow in its own shit all day, eating slop and getting fat. There's a reason why God told the Jews to lay off pork."

Uncle Will called us over to help scoot the pot of boiling water underneath the carcass. I tried not to smell the thick, musty air. Then Wilburn dipped Old Squeal in and out of the scalding water. "That's to loosen up the hairs so we can clean the hide." He picked up a long butcher's knife. "You ever had hog cracklins? Millie takes the skin scraps, rolls 'em in batter, and fries it all up in lard. Delicious."

Craw keeled forward. "I've got to lay down. That's as much farm livin' as I can take."

That night at dinner, I barely touched my food. It wasn't for Old Squeal's sake that I lost my appetite, though; I was worried about tomorrow. The reunion was supposed to be a great and happy day—food, dancing, talk. But to me, none of those things sounded fun at all without Sarah.

Finally, after rearranging my utensils seven times, I screwed up the courage to ask. "Do you think Sarah could come to the reunion? I mean, she's not a Henry, but—"

"Why, sure," Wilburn said. "I don't see any problem with that. You go ahead and invite her as your guest."

Aunt Millie's fork clanged on the table. "The Hawthorn girl?"

"That's right," I said. "Is something wrong?"

Her cheeks flushed. "I—I don't know if that's such a good idea."

I didn't know what to say, but Uncle Will spoke up for me. "Why the hell not?"

"The things they say about that girl—"

Wilburn held up his coffee cup. "Oh, don't tell me you believe all those rumors. She's a fine girl—just got a bad reputation, that's all."

I was confused. "What rumors?" I'd never heard a hint of anything before now.

Aunt Millie frowned at her plate. "I don't want to gossip. She's bad news, though—I'll tell you that much."

Uncle Will rocked back in his chair and sighed at Millie. "No use hiding it now." He leaned in towards me. "A couple boys that used to come around to see her, they died. Just accidents, that's all. But the way people talk around town—"

"There were three of them," Millie said. "Three boys. Dead."

I felt numb. "Three boyfriends?"

"Oh, I don't know about that," Wilburn said. "They were just boys that dropped by on Saturdays to see her, maybe take her to the movies." He took a sip of coffee. "First, there was Ronny. Poor kid stepped in a cotton-mouth den. Then there was Delbert. Damn fool dove off the trestle and drowned in the Brazos. The last one—I don't recall his name—"

"Lloyd," Millie said. "Lloyd Snoats."

"Well, unlucky Lloyd didn't watch where he was driving, and landed his Chevy at the bottom of a cliff."

Wilburn folded his hands. "Common accidents. Things like that happen every day. Sarah's had a string of bad luck when it comes to boys, that's all."

Millie shook her head. "Once is bad luck. Twice is a coincidence. Three times is a pattern."

Wilburn put down his cup. "What—you think she killed them?"

"Of course not. Not directly, at least." Millie lowered her voice to a whisper. "They say she's cursed. It's that Indian blood in her."

Uncle Will threw up his hands. "Hogwash. *They*—who's they? The ladies down at the Bluebonnet Salon, that's who."

Aunt Millie looked straight at me. "If you keep seeing that girl, you're digging your own grave."

"Pay her no mind," Wilburn said. "It's a bunch of old wives' tales, that's all it is."

Millie snapped. "Are you saying I'm an old wife?"

"I'd better shut my trap before I fall into yours." Uncle Will glanced at me and winked. Then he slipped his hand behind Millie's chair and pinched her ass. She leapt up and knocked her plate off the table. Mashed potatoes splattered on the floor. "Wilburn Henry! Look what you've gone and done."

It wouldn't be long till the frozen chickens started

flying. Millie grabbed the bowl of gravy and held it over Wilburn's head. "Well, you're an old husband," she said, "so what does that make me?"

"A kind, patient, faithful, long-suffering, beautiful wife."

She rolled her eyes, then dropped into Wilburn's lap and smiled. I was relieved—one hasty word could have set off another disastrous chain reaction. It's a valuable skill, knowing how to defuse a woman.

As much as I wanted to ignore it, Millie's revelation unsettled me. Three boyfriends dead? I didn't know whether to feel even more sorry for Sarah, or frustrated that she hadn't told me herself. Should I still ask her to the reunion? I excused myself to go outside and think.

✤✤✤✤

When I stepped onto the porch, Craw was setting up picnic tables under a canvas tent. "I hope you're getting paid for this," I yelled.

He waved. "I volunteered my services, actually—in exchange for a free ticket to the dance."

I stepped off the porch and ambled towards him. "You're really coming to the reunion?" I was surprised Uncle Will would let him. Did Aunt Millie know about this?

"Wouldn't miss it for the world," Craw said. "Who knows—maybe I'll find me a lady to take back to my shed." He tweaked the brim of his hat.

"I'm not in the mood for jokes."

"Who's joking?"

"I need your advice . . . It's about Sarah."

A grin spread across Craw's face. "I knew you'd come back to me. Now go ahead—ask me anything."

I took a deep breath. "I just found out from Aunt Millie that she's already had some boyfriends."

"That's no surprise," he said. "You'd better lay your claim before somebody else comes along."

"Not just one—*three* boyfriends."

"The competition is fierce, eh?" Craw raised his hook. "Where are they? I'll kill the bastards."

"They're already dead."

"Hot damn, boy—you win by default!" He slapped the back of my head. "So what's the problem?"

"Three. Boyfriends. Dead." I waited a moment to let it sink in. "And she didn't tell me—I had to hear about it from Aunt Millie. You don't think there's a problem there?"

Craw sat on a table and motioned for me to come over. "Listen, my boy. Everybody's got a history. Something they're scared or ashamed of. Skeletons in the closet, if you will." When I sat next to him, he looked me in the eye. "Now, don't try to tell me *you* don't have any secrets." I thought of the money and my cheeks flushed red.

Craw must have thought I was blushing over Sarah. "You love her, don't you?"

The question jarred me. What did it mean to love someone? "I—I don't know."

Craw put his arm around my shoulder. "Tobias, my boy, a girl like Sarah doesn't come down the tracks every day. You let this train roll by, and you'll regret it the rest of your life."

CHAPTER 24

ALONG THE PATH TO SARAH'S, I thought about love. Did such a thing even exist? The way of nature was self-preservation, not self-sacrifice. And the more I thought about it, love seemed to be nothing but a fancy word that disguised our innate selfishness.

Sure, I'd heard a few sermons about love. In my father's system, you were supposed to love others—not for their own sake—but to deposit coins in your own spiritual bank account. Works of charity were ways of saving your own ass from hellfire.

And I'd heard a million songs about love. Bing Crosby and those fellows promised to love deeper than the ocean and higher than the stars for eternity. But who can sustain that kind of emotion for a month, or a year—much less forever? The song ends, the feeling fades, and they're onto the next pretty girl.

Maybe the only true love was the sort for sale at the Pink Palace. All the getting and taking of love, without the fluffy words and empty promises. Fucking without the frills.

But if that was the only sort of love that's real, why did it depress the hell out me? When I had the chance in St. Louis, I hadn't taken it. And I didn't want that with Sarah, either. I was attracted to her, but I wanted to believe that my feelings for her went beyond sex and self-interest. Did they?

By the time I got to her door, my hands were shaking. *There's nothing to be nervous about,* I assured myself. *You're asking her to a square dance, not a waltz ball. Partners at a square dance barely even touch each other.* Then I heard my father's voice: "You might say it's only square dancing, but it doesn't take long to cut the corners off."

For once, I hoped he was right.

Rosalind opened the door. "Tobias—what are you doing out this time of night? Come inside and—"

"That's all right," I said. "I just wanted to tell Sarah something. It won't take long."

Rosalind ducked back inside. A minute later, Sarah came to the door wearing a white nightgown. I was shocked to see her in something other than black. "Sorry," I said. "I didn't realize it was so late."

Sarah stepped out onto the porch, barefoot, and crossed her arms over her chest. She glowed pale and ethereal in the moonlight, like the forlorn spirit of a Civil War widow. I had a sense that if I reached out to touch her, my hand would pass right through.

She cocked an eyebrow. "Well?"

"There's—that is—" *What had I come here to say?* I leaned back against the porch rail and focused on the toes of my boots, desperate to gather my thoughts. "There's a family reunion tomorrow." I took another breath. "And Uncle Will said it would be fine if you came."

"Mister Henry sent you to invite us?"

"Well, not exactly." I glanced at her eyes, then back at the ground. "That is, I asked if you could come, and Uncle Will said it was all right."

The hem of Sarah's gown fluttered around her ankles. "Just me?"

When I looked up, she lowered her hands to her waist. I could see the outline of her nipples veiled in white linen.

When I opened my mouth, no words came out. My bottom lip was quivering. "I don't like crowds," I finally managed. "I was hoping you could come, so I'll have an excuse not to talk to all those relatives I've never met."

Sarah folded her arms back over her chest. "So I'm the excuse?"

Damn it, I'd done it again. Why couldn't I say what I meant?

She glided towards the door. "I'll have to see. Mama probably has other plans for tomorrow. Goodnight." She didn't look back.

"Wait," I said. "You're not an excuse." It was no use—she was inside the doorway now. "What I mean is—the reunion is my excuse."

The door creaked, but I heard Sarah's voice from inside. "For what?"

"To ask you to dance."

The door clanged shut. I stopped breathing. Silence.

I stumbled into the yard, kicked the dirt, and cursed the moon. Then I heard the door open behind me. Sarah poked her head out. "Thanks for asking, Toby. I'll see you tomorrow."

Heading back, I didn't walk so much as float. Boyfriends?—bah. Curses?—who cared? Snapping noises in the grass? Nothing could shake me out of my reverie—not even a rattler.

Well, *maybe* a rattler. I jogged for the last leg of the trail, then climbed the farmhouse stairs and fell into bed, exhausted.

I dreamed I was riding the rails again, only this time, Craw wasn't with me. I was headed back to Michigan with a big sack of Father's money tied around my waist. The boxcar was pitch black, and the only sounds were the whine of the wheels and the pounding of rain against the roof. Somehow, I had the feeling of being watched.

In a corner, I thought I glimpsed the form of something darker than a shadow. "Who's there?" The black shape didn't speak or move, but it sent a chill down the back of my neck. I felt around until my hands grasped the cold steel rungs of a ladder. What a relief—now I could find another car.

I climbed to the top and opened the hatch. As I struggled onto the roof, the wind and rain lashed my face. I kept on my hands and knees, creeping along the catwalk, but when I reached the back of the car there was nowhere left to go—only the caboose, and it had a smooth, curved top.

I tried to turn around, but someone blocked my way. A black silhouette stood tall against the sky. "Who are you?" No answer. I held out the sack of money. "What do you want—this?"

A flash of lightning tore through the darkness and I saw him—an Indian warrior with eyes red as fire and a face like melting wax. I threw the sack at his chest but he let it drop. It tumbled open, unleashing a shower of coins.

There was only one hope. I leapt for the caboose and slammed against the roof, sprawling. My limbs flailed for traction, but there was nothing to catch hold of. I slid over the wet metal, faster and faster.

As I flew off the edge, my eyes snapped open in the darkness of my bedroom. With a scream lodged halfway down my throat, I struggled for breath. For a few moments I could still see the Indian's shape standing over my bed. Then my eyes adjusted to the early morning light and he faded away.

Damned old wives' tales.

CHAPTER 25

BY NOON SUNDAY, the farmstead was crawling with every manner of Henry relations—aunts and uncles, first cousins and second cousins, in-laws and outlaws. And I was the featured, freak attraction under the big tent: the sole progeny of long lost brother Malachi. Children pointed and stared, old men whispered, large women embraced and smothered me against their bosoms. I grabbed a brown bottle out of an ice bucket, hoping one beer would be enough to get me through the day.

Chatter and laughter filled the air, along with a cloud of cigarette smoke and the scent of roasting pig flesh. No wonder Father kept his distance from these folks—he was the only white sheep in the family. And what a family it was. After a few sips of beer, the names and faces blurred together—Verna, Maynard, Fanny, Homer, Eunice, Elmer . . .

For lunch, I devoured a piece of Old Squeal on a bun. He tasted a hell of a lot better than he looked. I taunted Craw with the succulent meat. "Come on—just one bite."

He turned up his nose. "I have my dignity. Besides, I've got to save room for beer. Why eat lunch when you can drink it?"

Around two o'clock, I started wondering when Sarah would arrive. Or was I supposed to pick her up? *Damn—how do these things work?* Just then, two bony arms seized me from behind and lifted me straight off the ground. I squirmed loose and turned to face a shriveled old woman half my height and twice my strength. She caught me again in her vice-like grip. "My own flesh and blood!"

"I—I'm Tobias," I said. "Malachi's son."

"I damn well know who ye are. Don't ye know me? I'm yer Granny!"

I should have known—her few scraggly hairs were dyed bright peach. To give her another hug would have been overkill, so I held out my hand to shake hers. "I'm very pleased to meet you, Granny."

Her hand felt like a skeleton's covered over with parchment paper. She squinted her eyes, searching around me. "Now where in tarnation is that boy of mine?"

She must have meant my father. "He's sorry he couldn't make it down," I said. "But the church, you know—"

"I ain't seen hide nor hair of that boy in damn near twenty years." Granny spat a stream of brown tobacco juice onto the ground. "You tell him to get his ass down here where I can whup it."

Then she pushed me onto a picnic bench seat and squeezed up next to me. "Now, child, let yer Granny tell you everything you need to know about your illustrious forebears." For the next half-hour, she regaled me with Henry family lore. Her front teeth were missing, her breath reeked of minty tobacco, and she yelled as though I were deaf—but I loved every minute of it.

According to Granny, the Henry family tree boasted dozens of war heroes, including six Civil War generals— all Confederate, of course. "If Jeff Davis had put a Henry in charge, instead of that fool Lee, you bet yer ass they'd be flying the Stars an Bars over the Potomac today."

Out of pure spite, historians never gave the Henrys their due, Granny said. "Do you know who invented the automobile?"

I shrugged. "Henry Ford?"

"Horse shit!" she screeched. "Is that what they teach children in those Michigan schools? Well, they got it backwards—it was Ford Henry, not Henry Ford."

Just as Granny was recounting the exploits of Ace Henry, fighter pilot in the Great War, Craw broke in from behind. He cleared his throat and bowed. "Pardon me, miss, but I need to borrow this boy for a moment."

I turned around and caught a glimpse of dark hair and a red dress. When I stood up, I realized it was Sarah. Craw stood between us. "Tobias Henry, I'd like you to meet the girl who puts the rose in Glen Rose, Miss Sarah Hawthorn." He put our hands together.

It must have been the beer emboldening me, because I bowed and touched her fingers to my lips. Craw poked me in the ribs. "I knew you'd learn fast."

Then he turned to Granny, who was stuffing a pinch of snuff under her lip. "And who might this lovely lady be?"

"Granny, meet Craw," I said. "Craw, Granny." I whispered in Craw's ear—"Just try taking *her* back to your shed." Craw grinned, tipped the brim of his white hat, and sat down in my place.

Granny gave him a squint. "How the hell am I related to you?"

"Well, now," Craw said. "Surely you remember Moses Henry, the great explorer?"

I didn't get to hear the rest of his story, because Sarah tapped my shoulder. "Your excuse is here."

"A fine excuse." We snuck away, walking so close that my sleeve brushed against her bare arm. "Especially in that dress."

Sarah tugged at the waist. "This old thing? Mama sewed it from some feed sacks."

I touched the sleeve. It was coarse fabric all right, but I'd never seen a scarlet feed sack. "How'd she get it that color?"

"Soaked it in wine."

"Better not stand too close. I might get drunk." I already felt tipsy.

Sarah put her hands on my shoulders. "Sorry—I forgot Baptists can't drink."

"They can't dance, either."

"So what are we going to do?"

I carefully placed my hands on her waist. "I'm a bad Baptist."

When Old Squeal's bones were picked clean, Wilburn, JP, and the others brought out their instruments and tuned up. At the front of the tent, a row of hay bales marked the dirt dance floor.

Uncle Will called out a "one, two, three," and the Golden Melody Makers kicked up a swing tune I recognized from the *Texas Stampede*. Wilburn strummed his banjo and sang:

> *Chicken in the bread pan peckin' out dough,*
> *Granny will your dog bite, no child no;*
> *Hurry up boys and don't fool around,*
> *Grab your partner and truck on down.*
>
> *Ida Red, Ida Red,*
> *I'm a plumb fool 'bout Ida Red.*

Sarah tugged my sleeve. "Well? Let's see your steps, Toby—"

My mouth went dry. I'd been expecting to square dance, which wasn't really dancing so much as sashaying around while somebody tells you where to go. I had no idea how to swing dance. I'd never held a girl's hand, much less held a girl's hand while moving my feet in rhythm. Not even the beer could save me now.

As she took my hands, I was watching out of the corner of my eye to see how others were doing it. Sarah swung her arms, stamped her feet, and rocked back.

I almost tumbled over on top of her.

"Silly," she said. "You're supposed to pull me back."

"Got it." I nodded like it was all a simple misunder-standing. Like somehow, I'd thought we were *supposed* to fall flat on our faces. Then I took her hands again, count-ing out the beats inside my head. I stomped along with her a few times, then landed my boot on top of her bare toes. "Shit—" she let go and grabbed her foot. There was no explaining that one away. I was a bad Baptist and a worse dancer.

Sarah bravely took my hands a third time, and by the last verse I started to get the hang of it. *Tap-tap, tap-tap, rock back . . .*

> *My ol' missus swore to me,*
> *When she died she'd set me free;*
> *She lived so long her head got bald,*
> *Then she took a notion not to die at all.*

> *Ida Red, Ida Red,*
> *I'm a plumb fool 'bout Ida Red.*

"You can twirl me if you like," Sarah said.

"Sure you want to take that risk?" My head was al-ready twirling as it was. Sarah let go of one hand, lifted the other above her head, and spun around under it. Then she wrapped herself inside my arm, turning till she bumped flush against me. Glancing down, I caught a glimpse of paradise down her dress front. Thankfully, the song ended before my body had a chance to react.

Sarah stepped back and tucked her hair behind her ears. "What are you smiling about?"

"You've got a nice form." The beer made me as bold as Craw.

She raised an eyebrow. "What's that supposed to mean?"

"You've got a nice shape to you, that's all."

She laughed. "I've got the same shape as a washing board, silly."

I didn't tell her so, but that was one washing board I wanted to see.

Why do girls always fret about chest size? The fact that a girl *has* breasts is the exciting thing—doesn't matter how large they are. Sarah's might have been on the small side, but they crowned her body like rubies on a delicate silver band.

Across the tent, I saw Craw leading Granny onto the dance floor. Were they really holding hands? Craw whispered something in her ear, and Granny giggled and slapped his chest.

Wilburn called out over the crowd, "Y'all feeling good?" Everyone cheered. "Then why not kick off your boots and stay a little longer?" At that cue, JP dragged the bow across his fiddle, giving off a whine that made the hairs on my neck stand up. Bass and guitars joined in, then Uncle Will's voice.

> *Sitting in the window, singing to my love,*
> *Slop bucket fell from the window up above;*
> *Mule and the grasshopper eatin' ice cream,*
> *mule got sick, so they laid him on the green.*

> *Stay all night, stay a little longer,*
> *Dance all night, dance a little longer;*
> *Pull off your coat, throw it in the corner,*
> *Don't see why you can't stay a little longer.*

Craw and Granny went whirling past us, hand in hook. Craw looked at me over his shoulder. "Why are Baptists against fornication?"

"I don't know."

"They're afraid it might lead to dancing." Then he twirled Granny till she crowed with delight.

Grab your partner, pat her on the head,
If she don't like biscuits, feed her cornbread;
Girls around Big Creek, bout half grown,
Jump on a man like a dog on a bone.

Stay all night, stay a little longer,
Dance all night, dance a little longer;
Pull off your coat, throw it in the corner,
Don't see why you can't stay a little longer.

To me, the Melody Makers sounded at least as good as the bands on the radio. Could Uncle Will be right that Father had the best voice in the family? I'd only heard him sing God-awful hymns.

After a couple more swing tunes, Granny jumped up on top of a picnic table and called out a square dance. We sashayed, do-si-doed, flutterwheeled, passed the ocean, and promenaded for at least an hour. Square dancing wasn't half as easy as I expected. While Granny stomped, clapped, and hollered, I dodged and wove my way through the traffic, trying to avoid collisions.

In between reels, Craw pulled me aside and whistled. "Your grandmother is one firecracker of a lady."

"Granny?"

He shook his head. "If only she and I were younger . . ."

I put my hands over my ears. "Don't talk about my grandmother that way—that's sick."

"Oh, I don't mean it *that* way." Craw put his arm around my shoulder. "I assure you, my boy—my intentions towards her are purely platonical."

By the time the sun started to sink, the Henry men had drunk too much to walk straight and the women had great rings of sweat under their arms. "Let's wind it down," Uncle Will said, "with an ole-timey waltz. Just like the good ol days." At first, I didn't recognize the song:

I'm dreaming dear of you, day by day.
Dreaming when the skies are blue, when they're gray;
When the silv'ry moonlight gleams,
   still I wander on in dreams,
In a land of love, it seems, just with you.

I held Sarah's hand and put my hand on her back. She smiled up at me. "Lead me wherever you want to go, Toby."

"I don't know how."

"It's as easy as sliding in a box," Sarah said. I mirrored her steps as she counted out the beats—*one*-two-three, *one*-two-three . . . It was easy, as long as I forgot about what my right hand was doing against the curve of Sarah's back.

Then Uncle Will started on the chorus:

Let me call you sweetheart, I'm in love with you;
Let me hear you whisper that you love me too.
Keep the love-light glowing in your eyes so true;
Let me call you sweetheart, I'm in love with you.

It was the song Father sang to Mama the day they met, the one that swept her off her feet. Only this time, I was the one getting swept off my feet. Sarah might not have been pretty in the usual way, but it was her little quirks that got to me. Her freckles, pointy eyebrows, the fine, downy hairs on her arms, the way she smelled. Other girls powdered over their skin, plucked their hairs, perfumed their hair. Sarah was a wild rose—graceful without trying, beautiful without knowing it.

Whether it was love, lust, or just the effects of beer and a wine-colored dress, I didn't know. But I was smitten.

CHAPTER 26

WE LEFT THE TENT ARM IN ARM, floating on the last strains of JP's fiddle. The sun hovered just above the cedars, a red ball melting behind into orange haze. As tired as my feet were, I didn't want the day to end. I touched the back of Sarah's hand. "Can I walk you home?"

"No." She pulled her hand away and walked ahead, then held out her arms like she was balancing on an imaginary tightrope. Had I said something wrong? She fell off her tightrope and looked back at me. "Let's not go home just yet."

She grabbed my sleeve and pointed towards the field.

"Come on—I want to show you my secret place."

I blushed at her unintended double meaning and followed her through the tall grass, past trees, over the rocks, and all the way down to the river. I wanted to tell her my own secret—that I'd first seen her here, from up on that rock. We followed the shoreline till we came to a massive limestone ledge hanging out over the water. Sarah climbed up on top.

I looked around. "This is it?"

"Almost." She helped me up, then led me a little ways down the ledge, where she bent down and pointed to an indentation in the stone. "This is what I wanted you to see."

"A hole in a rock?" So much for my hoped-for double meaning.

"Look." She pointed to another hole a few yards away, and then to another hole several yards beyond that. "Don't you see what they are?"

I looked at them sideways. "Ah, now I see—three holes in a rock."

"They're footprints."

I put my boot inside the first indentation. It was about two feet long, with three toe-like marks at the top. "Whoever left these must have had a heck of a time finding shoes."

"A dinosaur doesn't wear shoes, silly."

"Dinosaur?" I pulled my foot out of the hole. "Are you joking?"

"Nobody knows how they got here, but the Paluxy is full of fossilized tracks." Sarah put her foot inside the next one. "Some locals are cutting them out and selling them to tourists. But nobody knows about these except me and Mister Henry."

"You found them?"

"A flood carried away the top layer of stone last fall. When I showed them to Mister Henry, he wrote to a professor in Austin. The professor came up to study them and said they're at least a hundred million years old."

"A hundred million?" My mind couldn't begin to wrap around a number that big. According to my father, the entire universe was only six thousand years old—which was a lot easier to imagine. "How could a footprint turn to stone?" I asked. "Water always washes tracks away."

"Amazing, isn't it? It's a mystery."

"I hate mysteries," I said. "I want answers."

"What does it matter?"

Kneeling down, I dipped my fingers into the claw marks. "If that professor is right, these footprints prove the Bible wrong."

Sarah raised an eyebrow. "What does the Bible have to do with dinosaurs?"

"Nothing," I said. "That's the problem. There's no mention of God creating dinosaurs, or Noah bringing them on the Ark, or anything."

"Why would the Bible say anything about dinosaurs? They died out ages before it was written."

"But the Bible's supposed to be the word of God. And it says the earth was created in six days, and the first man was created only a day or two after all the animals—which would have to include dinosaurs."

Sarah shrugged. "What's a day to God? A million years to us might only be a minute to him."

"You sound like Craw." Were Baptists the only people who didn't understand myths?

※※※※

Sarah's secret place was older than I could fathom, yet fresh as the dawn of time. When we finished looking at the tracks, we sat on the ledge and dangled our legs over the river. Water trickled over a thousand stones and pebbles, tinkling like a chorus of wind chimes. Something rustled behind us and I spun around, half-expecting to find a dinosaur. Instead, a buck, a doe, and two fawns emerged from the trees and glided down to the river for a drink. They were smaller than Michigan deer, and so graceful; now I knew why King Solomon was always comparing women to does, and breasts to twin fawns.

Amidst all that splendor, I remembered something Craw had said: *Show me a man and a woman in love, and I'll show you Adam and Eve.* Right then, it seemed that Sarah was the only girl on earth, and I the only boy, discovering the world and each other for the first time. We were just like Adam and Eve, except that we had clothes on. For the time being.

Sarah glanced over at me. "Sometimes I wonder what's going on in that head of yours."

I blushed again. "You don't want to know."

"Tell me."

"Mostly I think about you."

She picked up a stone and tossed it into the river. "That's boring. I was hoping you were thinking about something important."

"Like what?"

"Why we're here. Or where we're going."

"For me, it's all the same," I said. "If I can figure you out, maybe I'll know where I'm going."

She looked up at the purple-blue sky. "Then we're both lost."

A couple of stars twinkled overhead. We watched in

silence for a while, then I slid my fingers on top of hers. "I've never told you this," I said. "But I saw you near here once, before we met in the field."

She pulled back her hand. "What do you mean?"

"I was up on a rock, over there." I pointed to the spot. "Drying off from swimming. You didn't see me."

"Why didn't you say anything?"

"I was naked."

Sarah smiled. "I wish I'd seen that."

My cheeks burned red. "Anyhow—I've always wondered what you were doing. You looked like you were crying, and then you fell into the water."

Sarah tossed another stone into the river. "I was going to drown myself."

She said it so matter-of-factly that I didn't have a chance to register any surprise. "But you didn't."

"I didn't sink, so I figured I must be a witch." I thought she must be kidding, but she didn't crack a smile. Then I remembered what Millie had said about a curse. Did Sarah actually believe that crazy rumor?

I put my hand on her shoulder. "Since that day— have you tried again?"

"No."

"What changed?"

"I met you." She glanced at me, then looked out over

the river. "You make me smile. And when I'm smiling, life doesn't seem so bad."

I scooted closer and wrapped my arm around her waist. She leaned her head against my arm, then started to sniffle. "Toby, I'm so afraid."

I smoothed her hair. "Don't worry—everything's going to be all right." I cupped her face in my hands and looked, for a moment, into those dark, sad eyes.

"I wish I could believe that," she said, and closed them.

I kissed a salty tear from her cheek. Our noses bumped, and then I pressed my lips to hers, soft, wet, and growing warmer with every breath.

She pulled back. "I'm sorry, Toby. I—I can't."

I turned away. "No, it's my fault. I got carried away— one beer too many." My stomach felt hollow. I let myself voice the fear I'd had all along: "I know there's someone else."

Sarah climbed to her feet. "It's not that. But—I can't explain."

"No need to explain anything," I said. "Aunt Millie told me. She said you had other boys seeing you."

"*Had.*" Sarah wiped her eyes with the shoulder of her dress. "They're gone now. And if you died, too, I'd never forgive myself."

"Hold on. Is this about that supposed curse?"

She stepped back. "I knew you'd find out. I shouldn't have put you at risk." She covered her face with her hands. "Shouldn't have let you so close."

I reached out. "Don't be ridiculous. You're not cursed."

Then Sarah turned and ran. She flew off the ledge and scampered up the path towards the farm, dodging trees and leaping over rocks. I ran behind her. "Wait—you're not cursed. There's no such thing as a curse!" She didn't look back.

I climbed to the top of the hill, then followed her through the grass. She turned down a dirt trail I'd never seen—a shortcut to her house? I was already winded, carried forward by momentum alone.

Sarah bounded over a pile of boards and kept running. But when I crossed the same spot, my foot broke through the boards and I fell face-forward on the ground. My legs freely swung beneath me—I'd fallen into some sort of hole, and I was slipping fast. I grabbed at the planks of rotten wood, but they cracked and split around me. "Sarah—help!"

I dug my fingers into the earth and stretched my boots against the sides of the hole to brace myself. Then two legs stepped in front of me. "Sarah?" I looked up and, for a moment, a dark shape flashed against the sky—the same silhouette I'd seen in my dream. Then the rocks gave way beneath my feet and I fell, scraping and sliding down a dark corridor. When I finally landed, I felt like I'd been hit by a train.

The air was dank and stifling. I wasn't the first unlucky creature to fall in; the place reeked of rotting animals. There was a lump under my side—probably a rabbit. The skin was soft and loose, and when I pushed it away, its bones made a clinking sound, like a sack of coins.

Then I realized what I'd fallen into: a well. *The* well. And that wasn't a dead rabbit, it was my father's leather pouch stuffed full of money.

Dirt and pebbles sprinkled down from above. Was that damn Indian still up there? Of course not—my mind was just playing tricks on me. Then Sarah cursed.

"Shit. Not again. Dear God, not Toby."

My heart jumped. "Sarah—"

But she couldn't hear me. "Damn it all, he's dead." She began to sob.

I took a deep breath and yelled with all my strength, "I'm not dead!" Then I fell back exhausted. Darkness swirled around me, the money pouch fell from my fingers, and the world went black.

CHAPTER 27

I AWOKE IN A WHITE ROOM, with light streaming in through lace curtains. I looked down at my body, draped in a white sheet, and remembered Sarah's last words: "He's dead." If this was heaven, how the hell did I get past the gate?

A hand touched my forehead. I looked up and saw Sarah, still in her red dress. "Toby, I thought you were dead."

"Maybe I am." I smiled and my lip cracked, sending a trickle of blood down my chin.

She pressed a wet rag against my mouth. "Now you're the one who looks like a vampire."

I was sorry to see that her dress was torn and frayed in spots from last night's adventure. On the nightstand next to me, there was a plant of some sort with long, spiky green leaves. Sarah broke off a leaf and squeezed some clear juice into the palm of her hand. "Just relax," she said. "Craw gave me this to put on your scrapes."

"Is that cactus?" With Craw, there was no telling.

"It's aloe vera—it's very soothing." She pulled the sheet down to my waist, and I yanked it back up. "It won't hurt," she said. "I promise."

"It's not the cactus." I pulled the sheet tight around my neck. "It's that I—I don't have any shirt on. It's kind of embarrassing."

"There's nothing to be embarrassed about." Sarah put her hand on my shoulder. "You got banged up pretty bad. We had to cut off your shirt and pants to tend the wounds." My cheeks burned red—I hoped to God I hadn't lost control of my bladder when I blacked out. She peeled back the sheet and dabbed some of the juice on my shoulder. I winced. "Did Craw give you some salt to pour on me, too?"

She rolled her eyes and started rubbing it in. After a minute, my skin did start to feel better—not because of the lotion so much as Sarah's hands. I closed my eyes and breathed in her scent.

Images from the night before came back to me in bits and pieces: the red dress, the river, the dinosaur tracks. Had I really kissed Sarah, or was it a dream? It all seemed so long ago. With a shudder, I remembered the broken boards, the earth giving out beneath me, the phantom Indian. Then I remembered the leather pouch. My pulse quickened. Father's money was the answer to all my problems—and now that I knew where it was, it was just a matter of fishing it out.

Aunt Millie poked her head in. "Tobias?" I yanked the sheet back around my neck. She walked in with a steaming plate of biscuits and gravy—my favorite breakfast. Uncle Will followed close behind, shaking his head. "I've been meaning to fill in that damn well for years," he said. "Just knew someone would get hurt one of these days. Thank God you didn't bust your neck."

Then Craw stepped through the doorway. I couldn't believe it—Millie had never let him in the farmhouse before. He tipped his hat and grinned. "Well, well, well. You're looking well, my boy—now that you're out of the well."

I pointed to the aloe vera. "Must be that cactus of yours."

"Or the cedar bark poultice," he said. I hadn't bothered to look, but I did feel something wrapped tight around my left leg.

As I took a bite of biscuit, Aunt Millie put her arm around Craw and squeezed his waist. "Thanks for bringing him up alive," she said. I almost choked on the biscuit.

"Don't thank me," Craw said. "Sarah's the real hero."

Millie threw her arms around Sarah. "I sure have misjudged you, dear." Then she looked at me. "She's a real peach, Tobias."

"We'd better let him get his rest," Craw said. "Course you should stay, Sarah"—he winked at me—"in case Tobias needs help getting to the john."

As I ate my biscuits, Sarah stared out the window. I wondered what she was thinking. In the light of day, maybe she'd forgotten all about that silly curse—after all, I hadn't died. Maybe I'd broken the bad-luck streak.

I remembered the heft of Father's satchel in my hand. There were a lot of coins in the bottom, but they wouldn't add up to much. More importantly, it was stuffed full of bills—rolls and rolls of them, it felt like.

Would I bring it back to Remus? As much as I wanted to keep it all to myself, it was Father's money. And as much as I disagreed with his religious notions, I couldn't bear the thought of him and Mama dying in the poorhouse. It wouldn't be a total loss—surely, he'd reward me for my labors. And with a cut of the money—just enough to buy a little shack—Sarah and I could start a new life together. If only I could convince her that she wasn't cursed.

Sarah stood up and walked over to the bed. Her eyes were red and puffy. "Tobias," she said, "I've been thinking it over." I motioned for her to sit down, but she didn't budge. "I've decided that I can't stay here. It's too dangerous for you." She looked away. "It's time to say goodbye."

"But Sarah—" I propped myself up on my elbows. "I'm still alive. And better than that—I found it."

She looked confused. "Found what?"

"There are some things I haven't told you. Things I haven't told anybody—not even Craw."

She crossed her arms and waited for an explanation.

"When my father left here twenty years ago, he left a stash of money—a lot of money—in the bottom of a dry well. Right now, my father's in trouble. That's why he sent me to Texas. And last night, I found it. I held it in my hands, right before I passed out."

Sarah sniffed back her runny nose. "Toby, you're not thinking straight. You hit your head and—."

"I'm thinking perfectly straight. Everything's coming together, and it's all because of you. I couldn't find it on my own, but you led me to it."

She put her hand on the doorknob. "I—I can't stay."

"Don't you see it?" I slid my legs off the bed and struggled to sit up. "You're not cursed—you're a regular good luck charm. It wasn't the easiest way of finding the money, but that's my fault—I should have told you sooner. Should have asked for your help."

"Stay away from me, Toby." She cracked open the door. "Or something will happen. Another accident. He won't give up. As long as I'm near you, he'll keep after you."

"He? Who's *he*?"

Sarah let go of the door, wiped her face, and took a deep breath. "The day I was born, my great-grandmother prayed something over me—an incantation. A spell for an Indian spirit to watch over me."

"Like a guardian angel?"

"Sort of." She came closer. "Only he's not much of an angel. More like a demon. He never gave me any trouble till a couple years ago, when boys started coming around. He's jealous, I think, and when any boy comes too close—"

"You can't really believe this," I said. "Uncle Will said those boys got in accidents, plain and simple."

"It always looks like an accident—just like you falling. But somehow, he makes it happen, I know it."

"How—you've seen him?"

"A few times, starting from when I was a child. Usually at night."

"It's easy to imagine things in the dark—I do it myself. Moonlight plays tricks on you."

"He's an Indian warrior. Strong and very tall—maybe seven feet."

A chill went up my spine. "With a face like wax?"

Sarah looked me straight in the eye. "You've seen him, too. I knew it."

"No, no—of course not. Aunt Millie said something about Indians and then I had a nightmare. Mental suggestion, that's all. There's no such thing as spooks, or angels, or demons."

She stiffened. "I shouldn't have said anything. I should have known you wouldn't believe."

"Darn right I don't believe. And if you help me get my father's money, you'll stop believing that nonsense, too."

"I don't want any damn money. All I want is for you to live."

That pushed me over the edge of exasperation. Everything depended on the money—and she was blowing our chance. "And you think *I'm* talking like I hit my head? Stop being such a superstitious ninny."

"You stay away from me, Tobias Henry." For the second day in a row, Sarah turned and ran. This time, I didn't try to follow.

CHAPTER 28

AFTER SARAH LEFT, I licked the blood from my lip and thought about how attraction is like a rose. It springs up from fertile, manure-rich soil; it blooms for a day, giving off an intoxicating scent; and then it wilts, rots, and festers on the shit pile of life. As my father might have said, all things come from shit; all things return to shit—except he would have used the word "dust."

A knock at the door shook me from my melancholy musings. It had the unmistakable ring of Craw's hook. He removed his hat, scratched his bald head, and awkwardly stepped into the room. "Tobias, my boy, I've come to say goodbye."

I dropped my head on the pillow—stunned again. This was turning out to be a bad day for goodbyes.

"My work here is done," he said, "and the road beckons onward."

I raised my head. "But the fence—"

"Son, if I stayed on till that damn fence was up, they'd bury me inside it. The cattle would graze on my grave. That's the last thing I need—a bunch of bullshit on my tombstone." He glanced up at the ceiling. "Then again, that might be appropriate."

Then I remembered the money. If Sarah wouldn't help me get it, maybe Craw would. "Wait a minute," I said. "Would you stay for five hundred dollars?"

Craw stopped, scratched his chin, then waved his hand. "I'm a hobo, son. If I had that kind of money, I'd lose my position in life."

I sat up and planted my bare feet on the floor. "Well, if you're going, I'm going with you."

He chuckled. "Boy, you could barely jump a freight with two good legs."

I looked down at my bruised and swollen legs, with Craw's poultice still around my ankle. "I'll get that money I told you about—I'll buy us both tickets. How'd you like to ride first-class?"

Craw glanced around the room. "What about Sarah?

Where is she?"

I put my hand on the night stand and hoisted myself up. "She's gone," I said. "Ran off crying, and she never wants to see me again."

Craw sat down and shook his head. "My boy, my boy. I never thought you the type."

"What type?"

"The type to run out on a girl. Now, *I'm* the type to run out on a girl. But you——?"

"Look." I took a careful step forward, still balancing myself against the night stand. "I'm not running any-where—she left me."

"If you let her go without a fight, it's all the same."

I sighed and lowered myself back onto the bed. Craw deserved an explanation, and if he was leaving, this was my only chance. "Listen," I said. "The problem is, she believes that she's cursed."

Craw snapped to attention. "Cursed?"

"Haunted by the ghost of a seven-foot tall Indian warrior. And she honestly believes he's going to kill me—that's why she ran away."

"Damn," he said. "This is worse than I suspected."

"You're telling me—it's plumb insane."

He waved his hook. "Sarah, insane? Not a chance."

Maybe Craw was missing something. I spelled it out

slowly—"An Indian spook. Seven feet tall. Kills people. Now, do you believe that?"

"Why wouldn't I? She's an honest girl. And as sure as there are good spirits to guide us, there are dark spirits to block our path. They can annoy, oppress—and sometimes even possess a body. Sarah's sounds like a particularly pesky bugger."

"You're both crazy."

"Nothing crazy about it," Craw said. "Sarah says she's plagued by an evil spirit, three boys have died, and you almost shared their fate. If I were you, I'd damn well listen to that girl."

The scary thing was, it almost made sense—and I couldn't shake the image of that Indian in my dream. I turned away. "It's all superstition. I don't believe any of it."

Craw shot me a glare. "What *do* you believe in?"

"I don't know. Only what I can see, I guess. And touch." I rapped my knuckles on the night stand. "The cold, hard truth."

He sat down beside me. "Tobias, my boy, there are greater things in heaven and earth than are dreamt of in your philosophy. If all that exists is only what you can see, you live in a pretty small universe."

"At least it's real, and not some dream world."

"Real? Only a speck of reality comes to us through our eyes. Shit—things we can't see are the only things that make life worth living."

"Like what?"

Craw hopped up and paced the floor, thinking. "Beauty. Poetry. Friendship. Joy. Love." He stopped and looked at me. "You can't see any of that. Can't touch it. Can't stick it under a microscope. Can't prove it."

"Maybe it isn't real, then. Did you ever consider that? Maybe it's all in your head."

He crossed his arms. "You don't believe in love?"

I looked at the door, wishing I could leave. "Talk about love all you want. From what I've seen, it's just selfishness in disguise."

Craw stamped his foot on the floor. "I'll tell you what love is. Sarah risking her neck to bring you up out of that well—that's love. And if that ain't real, I don't know what is."

"Sarah said that you pulled me out."

"With what—a fishing pole?"

I shrugged. I hadn't even thought about how I was rescued.

"After you fell, Sarah ran to the shed. She grabbed a rope—and me. When we got to the well, she had me hold the rope while she shimmied down. Then she tied the other end to your waist and held you the whole way, while I pulled the both of you out." He looked me in the eye. "Does that sound like selfishness in disguise?"

I squirmed under my sheet. Craw had saved my life in St. Louis, and now Sarah had done the same—neither of them expecting anything in return. Sarah's words echoed in my mind: "All I want is for you to live." Could I say the same for her, or was I just out for myself? Even if the curse was a fake, I shouldn't have called her crazy. But what could I do?

"I wish I could help her," I said. "But I don't know how. How can you love a girl that's haunted?"

Craw put his hand on my shoulder. "Tobias my boy, they're all haunted. There isn't a woman alive who doesn't have a demon of one sort or another."

I looked up. "How's that?"

"Remember your fairy tales—all those stories about princesses held captive by dragons? They tell the truth. Deep inside, every woman is a princess. And every princess has a dragon."

"First you want me to believe in demons—and now dragons?"

"Stop thinking like a damn Baptist. It's a myth, boy. And the point is, every woman is a vessel of beauty, life, and love—though most don't know it. And all the forces of evil in the world are dead-set against her. That's why loving a woman is the hardest battle you'll ever face. Love isn't going to fall into your lap—you've got to fight for it."

"You sure don't make it sound very fun," I said.

"It isn't—not all the time. A woman cries. She gets moody. Once a month, she bleeds out of her privates. Then you get her pregnant and—by damn, now you're really in a fix. You think fighting a dragon sounds rough? Try holding the hand of a woman in childbirth."

I began to see what he was getting at. Committing myself to Sarah—for better or worse, sickness or health, rich or poor—would be hard. I enjoyed being alone. I was comfortable looking out for myself and keeping a skeptical distance from everyone else. For me, even wallowing in self-pity had a certain pleasure. Maybe I was relieved—even glad—when Sarah ran out that door, because it was back to life as usual. The idea of getting mixed up with an unpredictable female scared me more than the thought that Sarah might really be cursed.

"If it's so hard," I asked, "is it even worth it?"

"That's for you to decide." Craw turned and looked out the window. "For most of my life, I didn't think it was. My head was full of questions, like yours. And now that I'm finally getting close to the answers, I'm too damn old to do anything about it."

It finally sank in—any other girl would be as much of a challenge in her own way. But I had never met another girl like Sarah. My choice was clear: find Sarah and face her demon—whether real or imagined—or spend the rest of my life jerking off to French postcards.

I pointed to the closet. "Throw me that pair of pants, please. And a shirt. I can't go fighting demons in my underwear."

"Or unarmed, either." He fished around in his pocket and pulled out a string—a necklace of some sort. At the end was a small bundle of red cloth. "Lucky for you, I've got a few tricks in my arsenal—or at least up my arse."

"What is it?"

"A charm—a talisman to ward off evil powers."

When he waved it in front of my nose, I knew right away what the bundle contained. "Fish guts?"

"Catfish heart, to be precise. I told you it would come in handy. Nothing kicks the ass of evil like a catfish heart—it's an old Indian secret. Why, one whiff of this could repel Satan himself."

"I can see why." As ridiculous as it seemed, I bowed my head and let Craw tie the string around my neck. He'd been right one too many times. Even if it was a sham, it made sense to use an Indian charm to fight an Indian curse. At the very least, it might dispel Sarah's fears. That would be miracle enough for me.

With the talisman in place, Craw placed his hand on my head in a ceremonial gesture. Instead of saying a prayer, he recited a poem:

> *I have read, in some old marvelous tale*
> *Some legend strange and vague,*
> *That a midnight host of spectres pale*
> *Beleaguered the walls of Prague.*
>
> *Beside the Moldau's rushing stream,*
> *With the wan moon overhead,*
> *There stood, as in an awful dream,*
> *The army of the dead.*
>
> *White as a sea-fog, landward bound,*
> *The spectral camp was seen,*
> *And, with a sorrowful, deep sound,*
> *The river flowed between.*

The hairs on the back of my neck stood up. *The river—* that's where Sarah would be.

> *But when the old cathedral bell*
> *Proclaimed the morning prayer,*
> *The white pavilions rose and fell*
> *On the alarmed air.*

> *Down the valley fast and far*
> *The troubled army fled;*
> *Up rose the glorious morning star,*
> *The ghastly host was dead.*

At the final stanza, Craw's voice swelled like the ringing cathedral bell itself. I gripped the talisman to my chest.

I buttoned my shirt and slid my legs into the pants one inch at a time, rough denim scraping against raw skin. Craw slapped my back. "I'm proud of you, son."

I snapped on the Lone Star belt buckle he'd given me. "Time to slay a demon."

"Almost forgot," he said. "The demon's only the first challenge—I haven't told you what to do once you get the girl's clothes off."

"Don't worry—I'm a fast learner."

CHAPTER 29

FOR THE FIRST TIME SINCE EASTER, I snuck out of the house, grabbed a fishing pole, and headed to the water. Only this time, I was after bigger game than bluegills.

I limped across the yard, dragging my left leg over the dirt. My body ached with each step, but the pain was exhilarating when I thought of Sarah. I even relished the sun searing my neck. What's a knight's quest without hardship? Everything good requires sacrifice.

Past the tall cedars, I slid down the bank towards the river. At the water, I bent down and washed the dried blood off my face. I hardly recognized my own reflection—cheeks swollen, arms cut and bruised, shirt soaked with sweat, pants caked with mud. I looked like I'd been wrestling alligators, not trying to win a girl's heart. But if Craw was right, they were about the same thing.

Rounding the bend, I spotted her on the limestone ledge, sitting with her arms around her knees, holding the rosary Craw had given her. When I called her name, she gasped. "Toby—what the hell are you doing?"

I held up the pole. "A little fishing."

She dropped the rosary and scurried backwards like a crab. "I told you to stay away."

"I came to say I'm sorry." I stopped at the edge of the rock—it was too high for me to climb up. "I'm sorry I've been such an ass. I should have listened."

"You still don't believe me," she said. "If you believed, you wouldn't have come here."

"I don't know what I believe. But I trust you."

She looked out at the water. "If you trust me, then go home."

"I won't let you go. Sarah, I'm here to fight for you." I wrapped my fingers around the talisman. If it radiated any power at all, I needed it now.

"He'll kill you."

"Not with this." I took off the talisman and held

it up. "Craw gave it to me—it's a charm to repel evil spirits."

Sarah came closer and eyed the red bundle. "It won't work."

I passed it up to her. "There's a catfish heart inside—it's an old Indian secret."

She took one sniff and pinched her nose. "You've got to be kidding. If you think I'm going to wear this—"

"It's for me to wear," I said. "Please—you've got to trust me."

She turned her back to me. "You'll die."

"You're right. I will die—someday. Everybody dies. But some things are worse than dying."

She bent down and picked up her rosary. "Like what?"

"Like never living at all. Or only half-living."

She fingered the beads a while, then brushed her thumb over the crucified Jesus. "Dammit, Toby—why won't you leave me alone?"

I dropped the cane pole and stretched up my arm towards her. "Because I love you. And I know you love me—or at least you did."

She reached down and pulled me up onto the ledge. At the top, my foot slipped and I tumbled over on top of her. I rolled over to keep from squashing her on the bed of sharp stones and jagged shells. I was already sore as could be—a few more scratches wouldn't hurt.

There were tears in her eyes, but somehow they didn't seem as sad as before. I cupped her cheek in my hand. "I want to kiss you, but I'd get blood all over your face."

"Tobias Henry, you're the craziest boy I've ever met." She leaned down and kissed my cracked lips anyway, entwining my blood and her spit, my life in hers, braving the wrath of hell.

Twenty years before, my father had thrown his life savings down a well, convinced that it was the devil's money. Now I was bringing it back up in hopes of saving Father's behind and kicking the devil's.

Walking to the well, hand in hand with Sarah, I thought about my parents. Back when they first met, were they like Sarah and me? Did Mama ever wear a special red dress? Did Father steal glances down the front? For the first time, I felt terrible for not writing to let them know I'd made it safely. I resolved to send a telegram at the first opportunity, and I imagined how thrilled they'd be to hear about the money.

I knelt down by the splintered boards and dangled

my hook over the hole. "There's a big one down here—just you wait."

Sarah laughed. "So *that's* what the pole's for. I was afraid you were going to hook me if I tried to run away."

I started spooling out the line. "Craw gave me the idea. He said he couldn't have fished me out with a pole—but I figured I could fish out the money."

The hook hit bottom. My hands trembled as I reeled in the slack. As I swung the hook back and forth, it snagged on stones and caught on clumps of dirt. Then it grabbed onto something solid. I gave the line a yank to set the hook, sinking it into the tough leather pouch. I reeled slowly, deliberately; if my line scraped against a sharp stone, it would snap. My pole bent and creaked as though I were hauling in a northern pike.

Finally, the satchel came into sight, hanging by its flap. As soon as it was within reach, Sarah grabbed it. "I can't believe this," she said, jingling the coins. "It's so heavy."

"Looks like the curse is officially broken. Must be the catfish heart."

Sarah beamed. "Let's count it."

"No—I want to savor the moment. Let's take it to your secret spot."

"It's not so secret anymore."

"I'm sure you've got other secrets up your sleeve. Or down your dress." I didn't need a beer to feel bold tonight.

She crossed her arms. "Hold your horses, Toby. I'm not taking you there till you put a ring on my finger."

"Then let's get married—tonight."

"The courthouse is closed, silly."

"Tomorrow morning?"

She only smiled. "Let's not think about tomorrow. Savor the moment, like you said."

I'd waited twenty years; one more night wouldn't hurt—unless Jesus came back. If there was a God, surely he could hold off the Rapture two more nights for my sake.

Back at the dinosaur tracks, I gathered some dead wood and started a fire—the one useful skill I'd learned on the road. The sky was deep purple and the air blowing off the river enveloped us in a thick, cool blanket. Fireflies danced over the river, cicadas buzzed across the bank, and a whippoorwill sang in the cedars above. Sarah sat transfigured in the firelight, her face and arms glowing as if illumined from within.

"I know you don't care about money," I said. "At

least, you didn't this morning. But there's more than money in this bag—it's our future. We can buy a car. A home."

"This is my home." Sarah looked into my eyes. "Right here, right now. Wherever you are is home."

I pulled at the satchel's rusty latch, and the brittle leather strap broke off in my fingers. Then I lifted the flap, revealing rolls and rolls of tightly wound bills. One by one, I stacked them in a pyramid before the fire; by the time I was done, there were twenty-three rolls on the pile.

I ran my fingers through the coins at the bottom, scooping them up and letting them fall in a shower of tarnished silver and bronze. "Have you ever seen so much money in your life?"

Sarah shook her head, a big smile on her face.

Each roll of bills looked like a short, fat cigar. I held one up and snapped off the twine holding it together. As I peeled it off, the first dollar cracked—then crumbled into pieces.

I peeled another.

Then another.

"No!"

Brown flakes floated through the air like the dead leaves of a Michigan Fall.

Staring speechless at the smothering rubble, I felt like a man watching his house burn down. All of that searching, waiting, trying to fulfill my father's wish—I couldn't fathom what I had just lost.

Sarah covered her face. "It's all my fault. It's the curse."

"Please—don't say that."

"But your whole journey—for nothing—"

I tossed the butt of my hundred-dollar cigar into the fire. "I found you—that's something." I wrapped my arms around her, put my hand under her chin, and lifted Sarah's face to mine. "You're worth more than anything." Our noses touched; her lips brushed against mine.

Then she pushed away. "What's that smell?"

I pulled off the talisman. "This?" I drew my arm back to toss Craw's charm into the river, but Sarah stopped me. "It's not that," she said, covering her nose. Then I smelled it, too: like a dead animal rotting in the sun. Was it that damn poultice of Craw's on my ankle? No—the stench seemed to be coming from the fire.

A cloud of thick, black smoke billowed out around us. "Must be an animal fell in the fire," I said. Sarah started coughing. I fanned my shirt at the flames, but that only made matters worse. Smoke clogged my nose and stung my eyes. Sarah gagged.

In an instant, the fire exploded and flames ripped through the smoke. The blast of white-hot light threw us back against the rock, searing our skin. I rolled on top of Sarah to shield her, then struggled to my feet.

A column of black smoke rose from the flames, towering above us. Slowly, almost imperceptibly, it twisted into the shape of a man's torso. Flames spiraled up the spectral body, flashing across what seemed to be a broad chest and thick arms. Sarah grabbed my leg.

High above us, a pair of red eyes lit up like burning coals. Streaks of flame revealed a face, bubbling and dripping like melting wax. Sarah screamed. I tore at my collar—where was the talisman?

The Indian stretched out an arm of smoke and flame towards me. As it came closer, the arm twisted into the form of a snake slithering through the air. It coiled in front of my face, singeing my eyebrows with its heat. Sarah held up her rosary. "Don't you dare touch him!" I squeezed my fist and realized that I'd been holding the talisman all along.

I hurled the catfish heart into the fire and yelled the first thing that came to mind. "Go to hell, you damn blasted son of a bitch!"

The talisman exploded in a great puff of white smoke. A screech pierced the air, and the demon writhed backwards, pulling the snake around his own neck. His waxen face stretched wider and wider, then collapsed in on itself. He sputtered, wheezed, hissed, and finally sank into the flames, vanquished.

As the white smoke flushed the black smoke away, our fire died down to its original size. The only sign of our battle was a curled strip of snakeskin sizzling on the ground by my feet. Sarah picked up the charred skin with a stick and tossed it into the river. Both dazed, we watched the demon's last remains dissolve to dust and float away.

Sarah put her arm around my waist. "Where'd you learn to cuss like that?"

I blew the ashes off her shoulder. "From my mama."

"I can't wait to meet her."

For what seemed like an eternity, we stood there watching the water ripple by. Then I felt something swell up inside me. No, not in that part of me—though I was swelling down there, too. I felt like a child on Christmas morning, my chest about to burst with excitement. Sarah was my gift—the best gift imaginable—and I needed someone to thank.

I pressed my cheek against Sarah's hair, closed my eyes, and—for the first time in months—I prayed. "If you're up there, thank you. Please grant us many years together under the same roof. And while you're at it, maybe even a baby."

When I opened my eyes, Sarah looked up and whispered. "Three babies."

Did I really know what I was getting myself into?

CHAPTER 30

FATHER'S MONEY wasn't a total loss. There was almost ten dollars in coins at the bottom of the satchel—just enough to buy two golden bands at the pawn shop.

Sarah was hesitant about the idea of a courthouse wedding. "It doesn't seem real if it's not in a church."

"The Bible says that the body is the temple of the Holy Spirit. That means wherever you are, there's my church. You're a cathedral." She smiled and let me carry her up the courthouse steps. For once, my Scripture knowledge came in handy.

Half an hour later, we were pronounced man and wife. Some people put more effort and money into the wedding day than they do into the marriage itself, then it's all downhill from there. I was happy for a simple start; things could only get better.

On the way out of town, I stopped by Western Union and sent a telegram to my parents:

```
MRS. ADA HENRY
REMUS MICHIGAN

=I AM ALIVE= TELL FATHER MONEY WAS
ALL  ROTTEN=COMING  HOME  SOON  I
HOPE=WILL THINK OF SOMETHING=

=TOBIAS=

=PS GOOD NEWS I AM MARRIED TODAY=DO
NOT WORRY SHE IS BAPTIST=
```

I left off the Catholic part. What Father didn't know couldn't hurt him.

Back at the Henry farm, everyone was surprised and thrilled by our announcement. Uncle Will threw his hat up in the air and ye-hawed, while Aunt Millie bawled and blubbered as if I was her own son.

I was worried how she'd react, but even Sarah's mama was happy. "I thought this day would never come," she kept saying. She hugged and kissed me and said I'd make a wonderful son-in-law, but I could tell she wasn't as excited about me as she was about her grandchildren-to-be.

I knocked on Craw's shed, but there was no answer. Inside, on his mattress, he'd left one last gift: a little brown jar labeled "Catfish Liver Salve." Was this Craw's idea of a wedding present? There was a note in his own handwriting:

Cures warts, goiters, liver spots, and scales over the eyes caused by bird droppings. Apply directly to affected area and rinse with warm water. Repeat three times.

Next to that, I found a red hardback book, *Forbidden Secrets of Sex Revealed*, by Dr. Herman Waldo Long. Good ol' Craw.

I finally came clean and told Wilburn and Millie about Father's accident and the lost money. I detected the hint of a satisfied smile on Uncle Will's face, but he offered to take up a collection among the relatives.

"Father won't take charity," I said. "That's why he

wanted me to keep it a secret." I didn't have any problem taking charity, though. For a wedding present, Wilburn gave us an old Model A that he'd been repairing in the barn.

"Only one string attached," he said. "Y'all hurry back to Texas. Don't go disappearing on us like your father." I promised we'd be back—and maybe I could convince my parents to return, too. As crazy as it seemed, I dreamed of Father rejoining the Golden Melody Makers and getting them on the radio. I could hardly imagine what it would be like to hear him pour his heart into a real, honest-to-God song.

Just as Sarah and I were about to leave, Uncle Will came out onto the porch holding an apple crate full of papers. "Almost forgot," he said. "Malachi's been getting mail here ever since he left. Only a letter or two a year, but it adds up." He packed the crate into our trunk. "Don't know why I saved these—guess I figured he might come back someday."

I looked down at my feet. "I almost forgot something too—your boots." I started to pull them off.

Uncle Will put his hand on my shoulder. "You keep those. No matter where you go, you're a Texan now."

We didn't get to make love on our wedding night, or the night after. The trip to Remus was a three-day's drive on hard leather seats, and Sarah's body was as sore as mine by the time we got there. Consummating our marriage was turning out to be a bigger challenge than fighting the demon. After all we'd been through, though, and with my parents' fate in the balance, sex wasn't the first thing on my mind. Well, maybe it was, but I did a good job of pretending otherwise.

When we pulled into my drive, Father was sitting on the porch with a red bandana across his face, strumming his old guitar. I was shocked—I thought he'd smashed it years ago. Mama came running out to meet us. They hugged Sarah and declared that she was the daughter they'd never been able to have. "The Lord has brought joy from ashes," Father said. "I'm grateful for all that's happened—even my blindness. My only regret is that I'll never see my grandchildren with my own eyes."

I was beginning to wonder if there'd ever be any grandchildren. No way was I going to make love for the first time in my old bedroom, right down the hall from my parents.

That evening, I asked Father what he meant when he said he was grateful for his blindness. "Ada was mad as a wet hen when she found out I'd sent you away," he said.

"She thought sure you were dead. To pacify her, I told her to fetch the Bible and read to me from Jesus' Sermon on the Mount. 'Blessed are the peacemakers,' 'love your enemies,' 'turn the other cheek'—I hoped something would sink in and keep her from killing me."

Father tilted back his head. "But as she read, I realized that I was the one who needed it. My eyes were opened—figuratively, at least—and I heard the words of Jesus as if he were speaking directly to me. The more she read, the more I saw myself—not in Jesus or his followers, but in the Pharisees, the teachers of the law. All these years I'd been fighting my enemies, I missed out on the most important thing: love."

He pointed to the bandana around his eyes. "I was so stubborn, God had to blind me to show me the truth."

In his moment of epiphany, Father seemed to forget that he was blinded by a bird, not God. Then again, Scripture says that the Spirit descends as a dove and works in mysterious ways.

The next morning, I brought Father the crate of letters Uncle Will had saved for him. Most of them were from the same place: "Artesian Mfg. & Bottling Co., Waco, Texas."

When I asked Father if that rang a bell, he had to think about it for a minute. "Now I remember. One of my friends convinced me to invest money in a new industry—soda pop, I think it was. Let this be a lesson to you, son—never waste your money on some fool scheme."

I opened the most recent letter. The fool scheme in question was Dr. Pepper soda. "Dad—it says here that your original investment of twelve dollars is now worth fifteen thousand." I dropped the letter in amazement.

Father slowly shook his head, then grinned. "Which goes to show you, son—don't listen to a word your old man says."

About noon, when Brother Lester and the Baptist elders dropped by to give Father his one-day eviction notice, they were shocked to find us celebrating. "Brothers," Father told them, "as the great Davy Crockett once said, 'You can go to hell—but as for me, I'm going to Texas.'" As we yipped and hollered, the elders tumbled out the door and ran away, falling all over each other like the Keystone Cops.

In all the excitement, I almost forgot Craw's catfish liver salve. That afternoon, I asked Father to remove his bandana, and I smeared the pungent brown paste over his eyelids. All I said was, "Don't ask what it is, but it might help." I rubbed it on and wiped it off twice, with no change in the cloudy white film over his eyes. Then, the third time, the scales peeled back, flaked off, and floated away like snowflakes. Father threw his arms around me. "I was blind, but now I see—praise be to God."

Maybe the Spirit works through catfish entrails, too.

That evening, after packing up the few belongings I cared to take back to Texas, I brought Sarah to the stump behind the house and dug up my secret lockbox.

I was a bit embarrassed to show her at first, but we both had a good laugh over the French Lady. "You kind of look alike," I said. "Maybe it's the black hair."

"And our armpits," Sarah said. "I gave up shaving when I swore off boys."

I took my page of hand-copied verses from the Song of Solomon, and we hiked out to the lake. There, we lay on the grass in the cool night air, and I read the verses to Sarah. Years before, when I'd written them down, they seemed so dirty. Now, they seemed the most beautiful and innocent words in the world.

When I ran out of verses about breasts, Sarah unveiled her own under the silvery Michigan moon. She lay beside me and we sang a song of our own, our bodies communing in a language more ancient than any spoken tongue.

Mama's health books had introduced me to the scientific side of sex, and Dr. Herman Waldo Long had given me a few helpful pointers. But those science and technical books didn't tell half of the truth about sex.

As Craw once told me, some truths are so big, so far beyond our understanding, that the only way we can grasp them is through a myth. Sex is like that. It takes a poem to express the deeper truth of the experience, the part that goes beyond what we can see. Anatomical drawings and Latin terms couldn't begin describe what I found between Sarah's legs.

Before that night, some parts of the Song of Solomon didn't make sense to me. Like this one:

My beloved put his hand by the hole of the door,
and my heart was moved for him.
I rose to open to my beloved,
and my hand dripped with myrrh,
and my fingers dripped with sweet smelling myrrh
upon the handles of the lock.

Now I knew what ol' Solomon meant by "myrrh." Sweet, indeed.

And so, on the banks of Leach Lake, I realized my life's ambition to make love to a beautiful girl before the Rapture. What else was left for me?

To make love again. And again.

And again.

Tarry longer, O Lord.

the end

IN MEMORY OF MY GRANDPARENTS

For love is stronger than death.
SONG OF SOLOMON 8:6

AUTHOR'S NOTE

This novel was inspired by the ancient Jewish legend of Tobias and Sarah, as found in the Book of Tobit, and by my grandparents, who met and married in Texas during the Great Depression.

I love hearing from readers, so please drop me a line at sam.torode@gmail.com.